I0615489

William Thomas Roberts Saffell

Hail Columbia, the Flag, and Yankee Doodle Dandy

William Thomas Roberts Saffell

Hail Columbia, the Flag, and Yankee Doodle Dandy

ISBN/EAN: 9783337091439

Printed in Europe, USA, Canada, Australia, Japan

Cover: Foto ©Andreas Hilbeck / pixelio.de

More available books at **www.hansebooks.com**

THE TURKEY DRIVER
of Mount Vernon.

HAIL COLUMBIA,

THE FLAG,

AND

YANKEE DOODLE DANDY.

BY W. T. R. SAFFELL.

More solid things do not show the complexion of the times so well as ballads and satires.—SELDEN.

BALTIMORE............T. NEWTON KURTZ,

No. 151 W. Pratt street.

1864.

PREFACE.

THIS work is no continuous narrative—no work of fiction or imagination—but a compilation of well-founded tradition, interwoven with extracts from the accredited history of our country.

The reader is first made acquainted with life and character at Mount Vernon in the last few years of Washington's life; when the great Chief is seen among his domestics, living in all his greatness as a farmer, without the least obscuration of his glory.

The negro is noticed because he necessarily crosses our path, not as a slave nor as a freeman, but simply as an historical character and informant; playing his part in the life, the song, the literature, and the history of the Mount.

In the work, the ridiculous and the sublime are freely mingled, because they do actually exist together everywhere; and a separation is impossible without violence to probability and truth.

No unchaste expression or obscene word is found in the book. It can be freely read in all companies, and will amuse and instruct both old and young. Its history is good, its tradition well authenticated and the imagination has but a very limited play-ground. It contains also a truthful history of our national songs, gathered from living eye-witnesses, and cotemporaneous writers.

CONTENTS.

CHAPTER I.

CHAPTER II.

CHAPTER III.

CHAPTER VII.

CHAPTER VIII.

CHAPTER IX.

HAIL COLUMBIA

AND

THE FLAG

OR

CONTINENTAL YANKEE DOODLE.

CHAPTER I.

*Mount Vernon in '98—Miss Nelly Custis—Venerable Africans—
Plantation Melody—Father Jack, the Old Fisherman—Billy
Lee—Kosciuszko's Lamentation—Old Tige, the Watch Hound—
"Stealin' Cherries, is ye?"—"Hawk Kotch a' Chicken"—Mose
the Cow-boy—Aunt Dolly—Old Vulcan, the Historic Hound—
"The Old Black Fox"—Scomberry, the Philosopher of Dogue
Run—Washington at Home—Indian Prophecy—Lady Wash-
ington at Home.*

MOUNT VERNON, in the last few years of Washington's life was of
greater interest to the United States of America than the well culti-
vated farm of the great Cincinnatus was to the ancient empire of
Rome.

Whatever of good government, pure patriotism, polished literature, music, or innocent enjoyment, was known on this continent, or
in the world, was soon known and put in practice at the home of
the great chief.

The year of '98, opening upon Washington, who was then as
ripe in honors as in years, may be regarded as the "Augustan age

2

of English literature" in America ; or, as the Augustan age was to
Rome, the time of Addison, Steele, Swift and Defoe to England, and
the latter years of the reign of Louis XIV to France, so were the
latter years of Washington's life to America.

The mysterious powers of sound, the voice of melody and the in-
spiring anthem from the choir, that have ever poured their holy
refrain along the banqueting places of earth, had the ear and admiration of the *thousand souls*, that harmoniously moved along on the
historic grounds of Mount Vernon, where the soul of the pilgrim
ever drank in the most glorious prophecies in melody.

But apart from the accomplishments of government, literature
and music, so characteristic of the age, we pause to record the notice
of a joyous centre of attraction in the person of one of the most
beautiful and brilliant young ladies of her day, reflecting wit, and
mind and beauty on every surrounding object.

All who knew Miss Nelly Custis, the accomplished grand-
daughter of Lady Washington, could recall the pleasure they de-
rived from her extensive information, brilliant wit and boundless
generosity. Born on the 21st March, '79, she was therefore, in '98,
nineteen years of age, and the lively centre of attraction to all who
knew her, both at home and abroad. She was a great favorite with
the General, whom she delighted with her gay whims and sprightly
sallies ; often overcoming his habitual gravity, and surprising him
into a hearty laugh. "These were among the poetic days of Mount
Vernon, when its halls echoed to the tread of lovers. They were
halcyon days with Miss Nelly, who was then young and romantic,
and fond of wandering by moonlight in the woods of Mount Vernon."

In the Spring, the home of Washington appeared not only a beautiful habitation for man, but as a place which angels might delight
to visit on embassies of love. Touching the lyre, we might very
truthfully sing of it,

"There was gladness in the sky,
There was verdure all around,
And where e'er it turned, the eye
Looked on rich historic ground."

At Mount Vernon, in the olden time, there dwelt with the great
American chief many a venerable African, whose long life formed a

connecting link between the then present and the great eventful past. Encountering but little of the corroding anxiety incident to the life of the white man, he lived to a great age, with the use of his faculties, and his memory remained active to a remarkable degree. His memory was the only journal in which he recorded the history of a century, and the volume from which alone he could read up the great past. Unused to writing, his memory was his entire dependence, and a constant exercise of that power strengthened it to a degree not often fathomed by the pale-faced European. His family being provided for by his illustrious master, he had no anxious care about the future. With every day's departing sun his cares also departed, and his nightly repose was sweet and refreshing, even with the earth for his bed and a stone for his pillow. The rising sun found him full of life, and ready for his labor. He went singing to his task; despair found no lodgment in his heart; and melancholy never marked him for his own. He was a warrior, philosopher, politician, historian and poet, in his simple way, and mirth, and song, and smiles sweetened his life.

Among these was "John Tasker," commonly called "Father Jack," the fisherman-in-chief of Mount Vernon, from whose lips flowed lessons of history, experience and truth, as he sat in his cabin at night, or in his frail canoe to capture the finny tribe of the Potomac. "Father Jack was an African negro, an hundred years of age, and although greatly enfeebled in body by such a vast weight of years, his mind possessed uncommon vigor. He would tell of days long past, of Afric's clime, and of Afric's wars, in which he (of course the son of a king) was made captive, and of the terrible battle in which his royal sire was slain, the village consigned to the flames, and he to the slave-ship."

The stars by which the fishermen of the Hebrides were wont to steer their little barks in the days of Iona s prosperity, and which were the horoscope of Father Jack's night watch on the Potomac, now appeared to grow dim as his frail nature began to sink in years ; for the time was not distant when he would moor his wave-tossed canoe of mortality in the harbor of heavenly delight.

Billy, the favorite body-servant of the commander-in-chief, who had served in camp during the Revolutionary war, still lived in '98, the "spoiled child of fortune." At the battle of Monmouth, on the

28th June, '78, this same Billy, "a square, muscular figure, and capital horseman, paraded a corps of valets, and riding pompously at their head, proceeded to an eminence crowned by a large sycamore tree, from whence could be seen an extensive portion of the field of battle. Here Billy halted, and having unslung the large telescope that he always carried in a leathern case, with a martial air, applied it to his eye, and reconnoitered the enemy. Washington, having observed these manœuvres of the corps of valets, pointed them out to his officers, observing, 'See those fellows collecting on yonder height, the enemy will fire on them to a certainty.' Meanwhile, the British were not unmindful of the assemblage on the heights, and perceiving a burly figure, well mounted, and with a telescope in hand, they determined to pay their respects to the group. A shot from a six-pounder passed through the tree, cutting away the limbs, and producing a scampering among the corps of valets, that caused even the grave countenance of Washington to relax into a smile."

Then, here were the basket, broom, and splint-bottom chairmakers, busy till a late hour at night, in preparation of their merchandise for the market at Alexandria; and the comic serenaders that would "pat juba," sing and dance, to the great annoyance of these rigid old mechanics and sages, who, in order to "hab a little peace," would 'casionally enforce their respective doctrines on both the mental and corporeal understandings of their noisy antagonists.

Reverting to a scene at Mount Vernon in '97, as illustrative of character there, Kosciuszko, the brave Pole, and the friend of Washington, suffering incarceration in a European dungeon, we hear his "lamentation" in broken utterance, as it rises on the breezes of the Potomac.

> "O'erwhelmed with a flood of despair,
> In darkness I sicken and pine;
> No pure breath of life-giving air,
> No beam of the morning is mine."

It was on a beautiful evening in the summer of '97, the sable choirs of Mount Vernon being in harmonious but solemn session, that "Tom Grundy," the venerable post-man of the Chief, that "light-hearted old wretch," that "whistled as he went," though sometimes the "cold and yet cheerful messenger of grief," rode up and delivered the post-bag to Washington, at the east front of the mansion.

At such times, the politicians, sages and *quid nuncs* of the Mount would gather around, apply the ear to doors, windows, or key-holes, and record the news in the journal of the brain. On this occasion, an unusually loud talking is heard at the tea-table, mingled with acclamations of satisfaction. Some pleasant news has evidently reached Mount Vernon. What can it be? Nobody comes out to communicate it. Peter, the superintendent of stables, stands near the west front of the mansion, longing for Frank, the master dining-room servant, to make his appearance and soften the agony outside. He soon comes with smiles, and embraces Peter at the door!

"What's de news, sar?" eagerly inquires the superintendent of stables.

"Kosciuszko's liberated," replied Frank, "and is about to visit America."

"You doesn't say dat I hopes, does you?" blunderingly exclaimed Peter, as he flew to spread the news.

Peter reached the quarter of Billy, the venerable body-servant of the chief. Lights soon flew in various directions, from house to house, up stairs and down, and to the summer-house and conservatory. Mount Vernon was *illuminated!* Loud shouts pierced the trackless air! "Washington, Kosciuszko and Independence," in the wildest discord, silenced the sacred song. Scomberry, the Sage of Dogue Run, arose with "meekly solemn eye" to address the choir; the "white ladies" came out to witness the scene, and "Kosciuszko's Lamentation" never more saddened the melody of Mount Vernon.

"Tige," the old greyhound, was the constant companion of Thomas, the young turkey driver of the Mount. This venerable dog had been the leader of the "pack," in the sporting days of Mount Vernon; was the oldest dog on the plantation, and, in '98, was the patriarch of the kennel. His hair had grown grey, and long years of hard service had dimmed his sight. When Billy, the old huntsman and body-servant of the Chief, would pat him on the head and talk to him of the chase in days gone by, he would listen as though he understood every word, and appeared to mutter out his regret that he was not still able to lead the famous pack of the fleet-footed companions of his youth.

1*

On a calm, clear day in June, when Mount Vernon echoed a hum of joy, and the distant hills of Maryland spread out a serene and silent shore, a small boy, attended by old Tige, marched out with a flock of hens and young chickens, in orderly procession, at the western gate leading from the mansion, proceeded along the road by the conservatory, and finally passed it. Along the line of march, a luxuriant growth of grass and flowers, with trees bearing tempting fruits, quickened life and charmed the eye. But, alas! how deceptive are all appearances, and how frequently are we stung by surprise, by bees that lurk in the sweetest flowers. Coming to a small cherry tree, the boy discovered the ripe and tempting fruit, climbed the tree, and began to help himself to the large and juicy cherries that hung within his reach. Old Tige laid himself down for repose, and was soon half asleep at the root of the tree; the hens and chickens made off, and scattered to different places, as fancy led them, while the boy, filled with delight, and *with good cherries*, forgot that he was the commissioned sentinel of the hour. During this suspension of duty by the sentinel up the tree and his dosing companion on the ground, a large fish-hawk, sailing up from the Potomac, "bounced right down 'mong de hens and chickens, and Tige sprung up and made arter de hawk jes as fass as eber his legs could *toat* him." He arrived at the scene of the hawk's hostile demonstration just as he was leaving the ground with a chicken in his claws! He jumped about "ten foot into de air arter de hawk," but could not catch him—he sailed off to the Maryland heights with his plunder, leaving the two sentinels much wiser by the exploit.

The poor boy, in his hurry to scramble down the tree, became so entangled by the snags that he made but slow progress in hastening to the relief of his frightened and squandered flock. At length, however, he made a desperate effort to jump to the ground, but his long gown caught a snag, suspending him from the tree, with head downwards, dangling in the air. Old Tige, still in pursuit of the hawk, had leaped the fence into the wheat-field, and the faithful old sentinel's head could be seen, "bobbing up and down," in the tall wheat, in his endeavors to "sight out" the course of the fugitive hawk. He whined, he barked, the fowls ran screaming to places of refuge, the boy cried in great alarm, and the shrill voice of a multitude of Guinea fowls, mounted on the walls, trees and fences, joined in the "discordant melody," and there was music indeed at Mount Vernon in that critical hour. Aunt Dolly, the superintendent of the poultry yard, moved by the unlooked-for uproar, arrived on the ground just in time to behold the hawk soaring over the trees on the Maryland shore, with one of her chickens in its claws! and the sentinel leisurely dangling head downwards in the air!

"Hi! Stealin' cherries, is ye?" exclaimed she. "Hung up de tree, ha? Ye looks nice, doesn't ye? Hawk kotch a chicken, ha? You hang dar for one *whet*, for all I keers. Bound I'se not gwine to take you down soon," and off she flew after her squandered chickens, which, by this time, had all disappeared in the tall grass, and under the wood pile. The poor sentinel had, at length, somewhat recovered from his fright, and was earnestly trying to extricate himself from his singular situation; but all his efforts were in vain, for the strong material of his long shirt defied a tearing off from the snag; nor could he elevate himself so as to reach a limb of the tree and climb upwards.

At length he hung quietly, now and then rolling the white of his eye and stealthily gazing around, in hope of discovering some means of relief. Soon, Mose, the cow-boy, as "luck" would have it, arrived on the ground with his lowing herd, adding base to the music; and, seeing the suspended sentinel, and the excited Guinea fowls perched upon the highest objects, apparently making sport of the sight, he came running up the road toward the scene of confusion, with long cow-whip in hand.

At first, Mose was inclined to have some fun at the expense of the dangling sentinel, but discovering his subject in sufficient pain from long hanging, slowly proceeded to take him down.

"Dis shirt must be made outen 'normous strong truck," said the waggish cow-boy, as he "tugged away" in trying to release the sentinel from the redoubtable snag.

"Dis no tow linen," remarked he, coolly; "it's flax linen, sartin. I can't tar you down, boy. You hab to hang here for a skeer-crow I sposes. Den de hawk's not gwine to steal no chickens, I bounds. Good mornin', sar. How is ye, sar? You feels happy, I hopes."

Thus leisurely and coolly the cow-boy harangued the sentinel, as he passively hung to the snag, hoping for deliverance.

"I specks I hab to climb up and lif you off de snag," said Mose, and thus saying, he began to climb up slowly, as though nothing at all in particular demanded haste; and, gaining the limb from which his subject was suspended, he soon "liffed him off de 'foresed snag," and let him fall about six feet to the ground. The sentinel rolled over and pleasantly showed his "ivory," by a grin at the cow-boy. "Specks you down now," said Mose, with a mischievous grin. "Dis snag's a 'normous long snag, sartin. I'se gwine to break you off, Mr. Snag; you might hang me some dese days," and, suiting the word to the effort, broke off the snag; and, losing his balance, fell headlong to the ground. The sentinel roared, and the cow-boy, seizing his whip, said, "how is ye, boy? I thinks I must tetch you up a little to suple your jints," and he vigorously applied his whip to the bare legs of the sentinel. A sharp race, "under the lash," soon brought the two youngsters in the presence of the grave superintendent of the poultry yard.

"Hi, youngster, you's down, is ye? Better waited till I took you down. I bound de hawks eat you fust."

As Dolly was thus berating the youngster, the wagoner and schoolmaster, Thomas Mason, drove up and dismounted. Dolly readily told him the tale, but the only comfort he gave the young chicken minder was, "he-e-e—yah, yah, yah," as he mounted his wheel-horse, and shouted, "jee up dar, Jerry, I'se off arter dat, sartin."

Old Tige soon returned from his pursuit of the hawk, and with sad steps came and took his seat in the poultry yard near his fellow sentinel—the fun was too great to admit of any anger, and the two delinquents escaped punishment, except that which had been administered by the fun-loving cow-boy.

Tige was an honest old hound, minded his own business, and was therefore much beloved and caressed by all the servants, and especially by Billy, the old huntsman; but "Old Vulcan," the French hound, many years younger than Tige, would steal, and snarl, and quarrel and cause numberless disputes about trifles among all the well-behaved hounds of the kennel.

"It happened that upon a large company sitting down to dinner at Mount Vernon one day, that the lady of the mansion discovered that the ham, the pride of every Virginia housewife's table, was missing from its accustomed post of honor. Upon questioning

Frank, the butler, the portly, and, at the same time, the most accomplished and polite of all butlers, observed that a ham—yes, a very fine ham—had been prepared, agreeably to the madam's orders; but lo and behold, who should come into the kitchen, while the savory ham was smoking in its dish, but old Vulcan, the hound, and without more ado, fastened his fangs into it and although they of the kitchen had stood to such arms as they could get, and had fought the old spoiler desperately, yet Vulcan had finally triumphed, and bore off the prize—ay, cleanly under the keeper's nose. The lady by no means relished the loss of a dish which formed the pride of her table, and uttered some remarks by no means favorable to Vulcan, or, indeed, to dogs in general; while the chief, having heard the story, communicated it to his guests, and with them laughed heartily at the exploit of the stag-hound."

There were many very old foxes on the Mount Vernon estate that had defied the fangs of Tige, Vulcan, and the whole pack for years. They were all grey foxes, with one exception, and "this was a famous black fox, which differed from his brethren of orders grey, and would flourish his brush, set his pursuers at defiance, and go from ten to twenty miles at an end, distancing both dogs and men, and, what was truly remarkable, would return to his place of starting on the same night, so as always to be found there the ensuing morning. After seven or eight severe runs, without success, Billy recommended that the black reynard should be let alone, giving it as his opinion, that he was very near akin to another sable character, inhabiting a lower region, and as remarkable for his wiles. The advice was adopted from necessity, and ever thereafter, on throwing off the hounds, care was taken to avoid the haunt of the unconquerable black fox."

"When I fust took up my 'bode in de house 'whar I now lives," said Scomberry, the philosopher of Dogue Run plantation, "I sot out wid de old 'oman to raisin' chickens, and one season I riz de bes lot dat plantation eber seed. One day de ole black fox, chuck full ob 'cumspyronndable instincts, sneaked right up 'hind de hen-house and 'gan spyin' around arter his dinner. At las he trots right round de corner, and walks right smack into de door ob de hen-house, and sot de hens to screamin' in de mos' awful kind o' manner. I jes' seizes my old musket, dat had seed sarvice in the battle o' Brandywine, and makes a forced march to 'tack de enemy for 'trudin' on my premises and passin' my lines. I goes right into de hen-house arter de fox, 'tarmined to be skeered at no kind o' varmint whatsomeber, and pulled de door suddenly shet right arter me, and 'gan to 'noitre round about in de dark arter de white of de enemy's eye ; but no black fox dar as I could 'scover. Thinks I to myself, ole black fox, you's not gwine to uptrip me dis way, for I'se bound to spy you out some whar. So I cocks my musket and opens de door jes' 'bout wide nuff to let in some ob de compound and 'centrated 'gredient ob daylight, and den I 'gan to 'noitre 'bout once more for de enemy. What in dis world do you think I next seed wid dese 'dentical eyes o' mine ? Wy, right in one corner ob de hen-house, jes right 'hind de door, dar lay de ole black fox, dead as a nit, wid de white ob his eye rolled over tudder siden his head ! I kotch him by de tail and gib him a mos' 'normous pull; but he made no answer 'tall whatsomeber. I nex' seized him chuck by the tail and toated him right outen de hen-house and frowed him down on de ground, so hard dat he went *kersmolloc.*

As I was standin' dar wonderin' how dis ole black fox come to his death, de ole rooster flew down from de roost, walked up towards de fox, as if spyin' round arter things, and said, Caw ! caw ! caw !

"I stood dar rejoicin' in dis heart o' mine, dat Mount Vernon was shet ob dis monster at las'.

He 'peared stiff 'nuff to be dead 'bout *two, free* days, and de temperyment ob de carcass 'peared to 'spress a 'gree ob cold 'bout two foot 'neath de zero, if de 'mometer was long 'nuff to say so. I soon 'gan to feel right skeered, and 'magined I mus' be gazin' at de ghos' ob de ole fox. I 'flected and 'flected on de subjec, and cast my eyes round on de trees and on de ground, to see if I want dreamin'; and den I 'gan to feel more and more skeered. I nex' started down to de spring to tell de old 'oman, for I swears I felt too weak from de fright to hollow for her, leavin' de dead carcas ob de old black fox stretched out on de ground, right 'fore de hen-house door. I walks down to de house, and sot my old musket down siden de door, and starts off froo de bushes to de spring; but who you 'spose I meet, but the ole 'oman comin' to de house ? Jes at dis pint, while I was about to tell de ole 'oman what's gwine on, I cast my eyes round to de hen-house and seed de old rooster standin' right in de door. I nex' turned to try to tell de tale I was gwine to tell; and while I was 'splainin' to de ole 'oman, 1 turned my eye jes' slightly round agin, and what do you think dese 'stounded eyes o' mine seed? Why, I seed dat same old *dead black fox*, riz from de dead, seize de ole rooster by de froat, swing him over his back at de fust toss, and *run off wid him like de debil!* I seize my old musket and let fly de ruin arter him, but never totched tbe fust hair ob his hide. Dis was de fust time I ever knowed dat dis crafty varmunt would ape de possum, by 'fecting to be dead. Soon as dat fox knowed I had sot down my ole musket 'gin dat house, he comes to life jes like a sneak and stole my game chicken."

"The domestic duties of Mount Vernon," says Mr. Custis, of Arlington, "were governed by clock time. Now, the cook required that the fish should be forthcoming at a certain hour, so that they might be served smoking on the board precisely at three o'clock. He would repair to the river bank and make the accustomed signals; but, alas, there would be no response; the old fisherman was seen quietly reposing in his canoe, rocked by the gentle undulations of the stream, and dreaming, no doubt, of events long time ago. The unfortunate *artiste* of the culinary department, growing furious by delay, would now rush down to the water's edge, and, by dint of loud shouting, would cause the canoe to turn its prow to the shore. Father Jack, indignant at its being even supposed that he was asleep upon his post, would rate those present on his landing with 'What you all meck sich a debil of a noise for, hey? I want sleepin', only noddin'.'"

"We were accosted," says Mr. Custis, "by an elderly stranger, who inquired if the General was to be found at the mansion house, or whether he had gone to visit his estate. We replied that he was abroad, and gave the stranger directions as to the route he must take; observing, at the same time, you will meet, sir, with an old gentleman, riding alone, in plain drab clothes, a broad-brimmed white hat, a hickory switch in his hand, and carrying an umbrella with a long staff, which is attached to his saddle-bow. That person, sir, is General Washington."

This was the same Washington to whom the Indian Sachem talked as follows:

"I am a Chief, and the ruler of many tribes. My influence extends to the waters of the great lakes, and to the far blue mountains. I have traveled a long and weary path that I might see the young warrior of the great battle. It was on the day when the white man's blood mixed with the streams of our forest, that I first beheld this chief. I called to my young men and said, mark you tall and daring warrior. He is not of the red-coat tribe—he hath an Indian's wisdom, and his warriors fight as we do—himself is alone exposed. Quick, let your aim be certain, and he dies. Our rifles were leveled—rifles which, but for him, knew not how to miss—'twas all in vain; a power mightier far than we, shielded him from harm. He cannot die in battle. I am old, and soon shall be gathered to the great council fire of my fathers, in the land of shades; but ere I go, there is something bids me speak in the voice of prophecy. Listen! The Great Spirit protects that man and guides his destinies—he will become the chief of nations, and a people yet unborn will hail him as the founder of a mighty empire."

"Let us repair to the old lady's room," writes Mrs. Carrington of Mrs. Washington, "which is precisely in the style of our good old aunt's—that is to say, nicely fixed for all sorts of work. On one side sits the chambermaid, with her knitting; on the other, a little colored pet, learning to sew. An old decent woman is there, with her table and shears, cutting out the negroes' winter clothes; while the good old lady directs them all, incessantly knitting herself. She points out to me several pair of nice colored stockings and gloves she had just finished and presents me with a pair half done, which she begs I will finish and wear for her sake."

The foregoing pages are descriptive of life and character at Mount Vernon in the latter years of Washington's life, when, on a beautiful day in the Spring of '97, the departing sun began to gild the lofty forest trees, which cast their long and well-defined shadows eastward over the magnificent lawn. Twilight soon came, and a golden sky smiled serenely, without an obscuring cloud, over the earthly tabernacle of the great American Chief. A warm breeze from the river invited groups of servants, skillful in melody, to the open air, and happy children chased each other around the peaceful mansion of the liberator. Smiling Spring had suddenly emerged from the chilly embrace of Winter, the moon looked down on the happy scene, and, in that hour, the "Battle of the Kegs," to the air of "Yankee Doodle," rode harmoniously on the breezes of the Potomac.

CHAPTER II.

"EARLY in January, 1778, David Bushnell, the inventor of the American torpedo and other submarine machinery, prepared a number of *infernals*, as the British termed them, and set them afloat in the Delaware river, a few miles above Philadelphia, in order to annoy the royal shipping, which at that time lay off that place. These machines were constructed of kegs, charged with powder, and so arranged as to explode on coming in contact with any thing while floating along with the tide. One of these kegs exploded near the city, and spread general alarm. Whenever one appeared, the British seamen and troops became alarmed, and, manning the shipping and wharves, discharged their small arms and cannon at every thing they could see floating in the river. Not a chip or a stick floated for twenty-four hours afterward that was not fired at by the British troops.

"The city," says a writer under date of January 9, 1778, "has been lately entertained with a most astonishing instance of the activity, bravery, and military skill of the royal navy of Great Britain. The affair is somewhat particular, and deserves your notice. Some time last week, two boys observed a keg, of singular construction, floating in the river opposite to the city. They got into a small boat, and in attempting to obtain the keg, it burst with a great explosion, and blew up the unfortunate boys. On Monday last, several kegs of a like construction made their appearance. An alarm was immediately spread through the city. Various reports prevailed, filling the city and royal troops with consternation.

3

Some reported that *these kegs were filled with armed rebels*, who were to issue forth in the dead of night, as did the Grecians of old from their wooden horse at the siege of Troy, and take the city by surprise, asserting that they had seen the points of their bayonets *through* the bung-holes of the kegs. Others said they were charged with the most inveterate combustibles, to be kindled by secret machinery, and setting the whole Delaware in flames, were to consume all the shipping in the harbor; whilst others asserted they were constructed by art magic, would of themselves ascend the wharves in the night time, and roll all flaming through the streets of the city, destroying every thing in their way. Be this as it may, certain it is that the shipping in the harbor, and all the wharves in the city, were fully manned. The battle began, and it was surprising to behold the incessant blaze that was kept up against the enemy, the kegs. Both officers and men exhibited the most unparalleled skill and bravery on the occasion, whilst the citizens stood gazing at the solemn witnesses of their prowess. From the Roebuck and other ships of war, whole broadsides were poured into the Delaware. In short, not a wandering chip or stick, or drift log, but felt the vigor of the British arms. The action began about sunrise, and would have been completed with great success by noon, had not an old market-woman coming down the river with provisions unfortunately let a small keg of butter fall overboard, which, as it was then ebb-tide, floated down to the scene of action. At the sight of this unexpected reinforcement of the enemy, the battle was renewed with fresh fury, and the firing was incessant until evening closed the affair. The kegs were either totally demolished or obliged to fly, as none of them have shown their *heads* since. It is said that his Excellency Lord Howe has despatched a swift sailing packet with an account of this victory to the court of London. In a word, *Monday, the fifth of January, seventeen hundred and seventy-eight, must ever be distinguished in history for the memorable Battle of the Kegs.*"

The *battle of the kegs* furnished a theme for a facetious poem from the pen of Francis Hopkinson, Esq., one of the signers of the Declaration of Independence. It soon became popular with Washington's army, and is mentioned by Surgeon Thacher as follows: "Our drums and fifes afforded us a favorite music till evening, when we were delighted with the song composed by Mr. Hopkinson, 'The

Battle of the Kegs,' sung in the best style by a number of gentlemen "

The following is the poem, which was sung in the Revolutionary
army to the air of "Yankee Doodle :"

Gallants attend and hear a friend trill forth harmonious ditty ;
Strange things I'll tell which late befell in Philadelphia city.
'Twas early day, as poets say, just when the sun was rising,
A soldier stood on log of wood, and saw a thing surprising.

As in amaze he stood to gaze, the truth can't be denied, sir,
He spied a score of kegs or more come floating down the tide, sir.
A sailor, too, in jerkin blue, this strange appearance viewing,
First *rubbed* his eyes in great surprise, then said, some mischief's
    brewing.

These kegs, I'm told, the rebels hold, packed up like pickled
    herring,
And have come down to storm the town in this new way of
    ferrying.
The soldier flew, the sailor too, and scared almost to death, sir,
Wore out their shoes to spread the news, and ran till out of breath,
    sir.

Now up and down, throughout the town, most frantic scenes were
    acted ;
And some ran here, and some ran there, like men almost distracted.
Some fire cried, which some denied, but said the earth had quaked,
And girls and boys, with hideous noise, ran through the streets half
    naked.

Sir William, he, snug as a flea, a guest of Mrs. Loring,
Dreamed of no harm as he lay warm in bed, and freely snoring.
Now, in a fright, he starts upright, awoke by such a clatter ;
He rubs his eyes and boldly cries, " For God's sake, what's the
    matter ?"

At his bed-side he then espied Sir Erskine at command, sir ;
Upon one foot he had one boot, and t'other in his hand, sir.
Arise ! arise ! Sir Erskine cries, the rebels—more's the pity—
Without a boat are all afloat and ranged before the city.

The motley crew, in vessels new, with Satan for their guide, sir,
Packed up in bags or wooden kegs, came driving down the tide, sir;
Therefore prepare for bloody war, these kegs must all be routed,
Or surely we despised shall be, and British courage doubted.

The royal band now ready stand, all ranged in dread array, sir,
With stomach stout to see it out and make a bloody day, sir.
The cannons roar from shore to shore, the small arms make a rattle,
Since wars began I'm sure no man e'er saw so strange a battle.

The rebel dales, the rebel vales, with rebel trees surrounded;
The distant woods, the hills and floods with rebel echoes sounded;
The fish below swam to and fro, attacked from every quarter;
Why sure, thought they, the *deal's* to pay, 'mongst folks above the
water.

The kegs, 'tis said, tho' strongly made of rebel hoops and staves, sir,
Could not oppose their powerful foes, the conquering British troops,
sir.
From morn till night these men of might displayed amazing cour-
age;
And when the sun was fairly down, retired to sup their porridge.

An hundred men, with each a pen or more, upon my word, sir,
It is most true, would be too few, their valor to record, sir.
Such feats did they perform that day against those wicked kegs, sir,
That years to come, if they get home, they'll make their boasts and
brags, sir.

This was fun indeed for the negroes at Mount Vernon, and they
made the song "distinguished" in the history of the Mount for nearly
twenty years, when the harps of the sable serenaders were forever
"hung upon the willows."

No wonder they "patted juba," and danced it; for, to them, the
idea was simply ridiculous, that the great Lord Howe and Sir
William Erskine, who thought they could measure swords with the
"rebel chief," would summon their officers, "pummel the drum," and
draw up in line of battle to attack a regiment of floating kegs at
midnight. But the idea that

"Dem kegs, I'se told, de rebels hold, packed up like pickled herrin,"

was transporting, and the comic choirs would "adjine" for the night
with a "bust" of enthusiasm.

In Thacher's military journal we find the following account of the origin of the word *Yankee*, and of the phrase *Yankee* Doodle: "A farmer of Cambridge, Massachusetts, named Jonathan Hastings, who lived about the year 1713, used it as a favorite cant word to express excellence, as a *Yankee* good horse, or *Yankee* good cider. The students of the college, hearing him use it a great deal, adopted it, and called him *Yankee Jonathan;* and as he was rather a weak man, the students, when they wished to denote a character of that kind, would call him *Yankee Jonathan.* Like other cant words, it spread, and came finally to be applied to the New Englanders as a term of reproach.

Mr. Lossing, in his Field Book, writes as follows : "The air Nancy Dawson, as well as the style of words, antedates the American Revolution by at least a century and a quarter. A song composed in derision of Cromwell by a loyal poet, commenced with,

> 'Nankey Doodle came to town,
> Riding on a pony ;
> With a feather in his hat,
> Upon a macaroni.'

A 'doodle' is defined in the old English dictionaries, to be a 'sorry trifling fellow,' and the term was applied to Cromwell in that sense. A macaroni was a knot, on which the feather was fastened. In a satirical poem accompanying a caricature of William Pitt in 1766, in which he appears on stilts, the following verse occurs:

> 'Stamp act ! le diable ! dat is de job, sir,
> Dat is in de stiltman's nob, sir ;
> To be America's nabob, sir,
> Doodle, noodle, do.' "

"Long before our Revolution, the air was known in New England as 'Lydia Fisher's jig,' and among other words was the verse,

> 'Lucy Locket lost her pocket,
> Lydia Fisher found it ;
> Not a bit of money in it,
> Only binding round it.' "

"A surgeon in the British army in Albany, in 1755, composed a song to that air, in derision of the uncouth appearance of the New

3*

England troops assembled there, and called it *Yankey*, instead of *Nankey Doodle.* The air was popular as martial music; and when in 1768, British troops arrived in Boston harbor, the 'Yankee Doodle tune,' says a writer at that time, 'was the capital piece in the band of music at Castle William.' The change in the spelling of *Yankey* was not made until after the Revolution. Trumbull, in his M'Fingal, uses the original orthography. While the British were yet in Boston, after the arrival of Washington at Cambridge in 1775, some poet among them wrote the following piece, in derision of the New England people. This is the original Yankee Doodle song of the Revolution."

Father and I went down to camp, along with Captain Goodwin;
Where we see the men and boys, as thick as hasty puddin'.
There was Captain Washington, upon a slapping stallion;
And giving orders to his men—I guess there was a million.

And then the feathers on his hat, they looked so tarnal fine, ah;
I wanted *pockily* to get, to give to my Jemima.
And then he had a *swampin'* gun, big as a log of maple,
On a *deuced* little cart—a load for daddy's cattle.

And every time they fired it off it took a horn of powder,
And made a noise like daddy's gun, only a nation louder.
I went as near to it myself as Jacob's *underpinnin*,
And daddy went as near again—I thought the *deuce* was in him.

Cousin Simon grew so bold, I thought he would have cocked it;
It scared me so I shrinked off, and hung by daddy's pocket.
And there I seed a pumpkin shell as big as mother's basin,
And every time they touched it off they scampered like the nation.

And there I seed a little keg, its heads were made of leather;
They knocked upon it with their sticks to call the men together.
And then they *fifed away like fun,* and played on *corn-stalk fiddles;*
And some had ribbons red as blood all round about their middles.

The troopers, too, would gallop up, and fire right in their faces;
It scared me almost half to death to see them run sich races.
Old Uncle Sam come then to change some pancakes and some onions,
For 'lasses cakes, to carry home to give his wife and young ones.

I seed another *snarl* of men, a digging graves they told me ;
So tarnal long, so tarnal deep, they 'tended they should hold me.
It scared me so, I *hooked* it off, nor slept as I remember,
Nor turned about till I got home, locked up in mother's chamber."

The following song, called "Adam's Fall," sung to the tune of
Yankee Doodle, was composed by the British in derision of Washington, in 1775 ; but on the surrender of the Hessians at Trenton
in 1776, it was thrust back on its authors by Will Lee and his peers
to the sound of "Juba," in the hearing of the prisoners.

When Congress *sont* great Washington,
    All clothed in power and breeches,
To meet old Britain's warlike sons,
    And make some rebel speeches ;

'Twas then he took his gloomy way,
    Astride his dapple donkeys,
And traveled well both night and day,
    Until he reached the Yankees.

The women ran, de darkies, too,
    And all de bells dey tolled,
For Britain's sons by doodle doo,
    Were sure to be consoled.

Old mother Hancock, wid a pan
    All crowded full o' butter,
Unto de lonely Georgius ran,
    And added to de splutter.

De rebel clowns, oh, what a sight
    For awkward was dar figger ;
'Twas yonder stood a pious wight,
    And here and dar a *nigger*."

At the surrender of Burgoyne in 1777, "General Gates was informed of the approach of Burgoyne, and with his staff met him at
the head of his camp about a mile south of the Fish Creek, Burgoyne in a rich uniform of scarlet and gold, and Gates in a plain

blue frock-coat. When within about a sword's length, they reined up and halted. Colonel Wilkinson then named the gentlemen, and General Burgoyne raising his hat gracefully, said, 'The fortune of war, General Gates, has made me your prisoner.' The victor promptly replied, 'I shall always be ready to bear testimony that it has not been through any fault of your excellency.' The other officers were introduced in turn, and the whole party repaired to Gates's headquarters, where a sumptuous dinner was served. After dinner the American army was drawn up in parallel lines on each side of the road, extending nearly a mile. Between these victorious troops the British army, with light infantry in front, and escorted by a company of light dragoons, preceded by two mounted officers bearing the American flag, marched to the lively tune of *Yankee Doodle*.''

The foregoing gives an idea of the Yankee Doodle of the Revolution, which continued without material change, or addition to the number of songs, until the French war cloud arose in 1798, when the sentiment of Yankee Doodle became changed to suit the times.

"In this year, Washington was again awakened from his sweet dream of peace in his home on the Potomac, by the call of his country to lend to it once more his voice and his arm. There were signs of war in the political firmament. France, once the ally of the United States, assumed the attitude of an enemy. The king and queen of that unhappy country had been murdered at the command of a popular tribunal. Out of the anarchy that ensued had been evolved a government in which supreme power was vested in five men called a Directory."

"The French Directory assumed a tone of incomparable insolence, and the American representatives in Paris were insulted. Three judicious men had been sent to adjust all difficulties with the French government. They were refused an audience with the Directory, unless they would agree to pay a large sum into the French treasury.

" '*Millions for defence, but not one cent for tribute,*' said Charles Coatsworth Pinckney, one of the American Envoys; and he and John Marshall, another of the envoys, were ordered out of the country."

Almost three quarters of a century has rolled away since these words were uttered to the insolent Directory of France, and though, to perpetuate their memory, we often see a copper coin stamped, "Not one cent," yet the history of Mr. Pinckney's laconic speech has almost been forgotten in America. In these latter days we have not frequently seen those words on our banners and transparencies in processions; nor have we but once seen them "paraphrased" or "played upon" like other words in the same category.

It was not until the beginning of our present troubles in the United States, when "Yankee Doodle" was at a discount, and "Hail Columbia" under a temporary obscuration, that a certain politician forsook the flag of his country in a certain dark hour of its history; and though he did not throw stones at the flag himself, yet, like Saul of Tarsus, he stood by and held the garments of those who did. But when the flag in this politician's locality began to show signs of life once more, and stream majestically from numerous poles around him, he ignored all stoning parties, offered himself as a candidate for sheriff, hitched up "Old Fig" to his wagon, and conveyed wagon loads of his peers to the convention to nominate him.

The opponent of this would-be sheriff meeting him in the road with his wagon-load of nominating patriots, and referring to Mr. Pinckney's short speech in France and to a certain hour when the flag of his country was about to suffer martyrdom, he proclaimed in the ears of "Old Fig's" living load, and the candidate for sheriff— *"Wagon loads for sheriff, but not one man for his country !"*

The following is a specimen of the Yankee Doodle of 1798:

There's Ichabod is come to town from Philadelphy city;
He's strowled the streets all up and down, and brought nice tales
    to fit ye !
He's been among the *peoplish* folks, and vows them *rotten* clever.
They talk so cute and crack sich jokes, that make you stare for-
    ever.

        Yankee doodle, doodle, do,
        Yankee doodle dandy ;
        When times look blue,
        The hearts that's true,
        Are sweet as treackle candy,

Our tried old chief is coming forth again to lead and save us,
Again to show his strength and worth, when foes insult and brave
us ;
Our nation's boast—his name is host: let foes and traitors fear
him ;
Be Washington each patriot's toast, then rise to hail and cheer him.

Yankee doodle, doodle, do,
Yankee doodle dandy ;
When times are blue,
The heart that's true
Is sweet as 'lasses candy.

Yankee doodle, be divine,
Yankee doodle dandy ;
Beneath the fig-tree and the vine,
Sing Yankee doodle dandy.

The Yankee Doodle of the Revolution, and of 1798, were also the
Yankee Doodle of the war of 1812.   No change having taken place
except in the marine department of the United States, and this was
as follows :

Yankee land is Liberty,
Yankee doodle dandy ;
Let British boatswains wind the call—
Freedom is the dandy.

But Geo. P. Morris, Esq., our lyric poet, has recently immortal-
ized the Yankee Doodle of all ages, by the following pleasing song,
adapted to the air :

Once on a time old Jonny Bull flew in a raging fury,
And swore that Jonathan should have no trials, sir, by jury ;
That no elections should be held across the briny waters ;
And now, said he, I'll tax the tea of all his sons and daughters.
Then down he sate, in burly state, and blustered like a grandee,
And in derision made a tune, called Yankee doodle dandy.
Yankee doodle—these are facts—Yankee doodle dandy ;
My son of wax, your tea I'll tax : *you* Yankee doodle dandy.

John sent the tea from o'er the sea, with heavy duties rated ;
But whether hyson or bohea I never heard it stated ;
Then Jonathan to pout began—he laid a strong embargo—
I'll drink no tea, by Jove, so he threw overboard the cargo.
Then Jonny sent a regiment, big words and looks to bandy ;
Whose martial band, when near the land, played Yankee doodle
 dandy.
Yankee doodle, keep it up, Yankee doodle dandy ;
I'll poison with a tax your cup ; *you* Yankee doodle dandy.

A long war then they had, in which John was at last defeated,
And Yankee doodle was the march to which his troops retreated ;
Cute Jonathan, to see them fly, could not restrain his laughter ;
That tune, said he, suits to a T—I'll sing it ever after.
Old Jonny's face, to his disgrace, was flushed with beer and brandy
E'en while he swore to sing no more this Yankee doodle dandy.
Yankee doodle, ho, ha, he—Yankee doodle dandy ;
We kept the *tune,* but not the *tea*—Yankee doodle dandy.

I've told you now the origin of this most lively ditty,
Which Jonny Bull dislikes as dull and stupid—what a pity !
With "Hail Columbia" it is sung, in chorus full and hearty—
On land and main we breathe the strain John made for his tea
 party.
No matter how we rhyme the words, the music speaks them handy
And where's the fair can't sing the air of Yankee doodle dandy.
Yankee doodle, firm and true, Yankee doodle dandy,
Yankee doodle, doodle do, Yankee doodle dandy.

CHAPTER III.

*Mount Vernon in '97—Aunt Phillis—Billy Lee—The Turkey Driver
Belated—Old Tige, the Hound—"What dat hit me on de
Nose?"—"Sumpin' gwine to happen"—Phillis and Dolly in
trouble—"Caty did"—"Caty did not"—"O, what will Marse
say?"—Turkeys Lost!—"Lor! Marse might ax me sumpin"—
Council Fire Kindled—Assembled Wisdom—"Tarkeys all done
gone"—Sambo, the Cobbler—Search for the Turkeys—Procession
of Ghosts—Speech in the Wilderness—"Conscript Fathers!"—
"'Bacca Hills"—"Horn-blowers"—Scomberry's Poetie Philosophy.*

It was now about four o'clock at Mount Vernon on a calm, warm
evening in August, 1797. The dinner dishes had been "washed
up," and the servants began to visit each other, as was the custom,
until it was time to return and "put on" the melodious tea-kettle.

Seated on the steps of Aunt Phillis's cottage, was Billy Lee, the
venerable body-servant of the chief, with broad straw hat, styled a
"continental beaver," in hand, ever and anon striking at the flies,
and putting a host to flight. Aunt Dolly had been on a visit to
Aunt Phillis, both for business and an evening chat. Conversation
between Billy and Aunt Phillis had "fagged;" the grating knitting
needle, with the hum of the host of flies, was all that disturbed repose; and the old lady began to nod over her knitting, and Billy
fell into a sound sleep. Their repose remained undisturbed until
the slow degrees of motion had brought the hour hand nearly down
to six, and the lofty fir trees had cast their sombre shadows far across
the lawn.

Aunt Phillis was the kind mother of several sprightly boys; and

> "In the clear heaven of her parental eye,
> An angel-guard of loves and graces lie;
> Around her knees domestic duties meet,
> And fireside pleasures gambol at her feet."

Her child, in charge of the largest flock of turkeys ever raised at Mount Vernon, has not returned home from his daily drive ; but is three hours behind his usual time. Old Tige, the watch-hound, is not with the flock and its driver to-day ; consequently, she is anxious as to his fate ; yet she diligently plies her knitting needles till she falls into a troubled sleep. The harmony of the most harmonious of all places is about to be disturbed, and troubled dreams agitate the half-quiescent mind of the dreamer.

"What dat hit me on de nose ?" exclaimed Aunt Phillis, as she dropped her knitting and sprang to her feet.

"What dat hit me on de nose, I axes ?" she repeated, with eyes restlessly rolling around on every object. "Sumpin gwine to happen dis day."

"Nothin' hit you on de nose, as I sees," said the venerable body-servant, rousing from his slumber and scratching his head.

"I tells you sumpin did hit me on de nose," she repeated, "and sumpin gwine to happen on dis plantation dis day. I 'stinctly 'cognizes dat fac."

Billy laughed heartily at the expense of Aunt Phillis, and reaching after his hat, that had fallen from his hand, he hobbled across the road, and resumed his nap under the spreading shade trees.

Left alone to her reflections, she began "brewing" the most unpleasant thoughts over this affair of the nose; and flaky footfalls of dread began to haunt her very being. She became firmer and firmer in the belief that something did strike her on the nose ; and though she appeared to be sensible that she lived in the "golden age" of African philosophy at Mount Vernon, yet she thought such a strange circumstance could not be otherwise intended by some mysterious monitor, than to warn her of some swiftly approaching calamity. She stood in her doorway, anxiously looking for the drove of turkeys to make its appearance over the hills, and then at Billy unconsciously snoring on the grass ; and wondered how he could be so lost to all impression as to leave her alone and without counsel in that hour of trouble.

She beheld "the hands," in small squads, returning from their labor, and singing their ever-cheering songs of contentment. With confidence she looked to hear from some of the returning servants a narrative of some sad calamity that had occurred on the plantation

4

that day; but all came singing in joyous song, till every one had arrived at his respective quarters for the night. She now concluded that her child, the turkey driver, only eleven years of age, and his flock of more than one hundred, were in some terrible distress, perhaps wandered too far and lost the way home; and she, therefore, began to lose her resolution, and sink into "oceans of trouble." Seven o'clock on an evening in August came, and threatening clouds came with the hour, and foreshadowed a storm; but the child and his flock did not appear. Aunt Dolly, the superintendent of the poultry yard, had all the other fowls in their respective places for the night, and, like Aunt Phillis, stood silently looking for the flock, with many evil surmisings. She felt that the flock had been alarmingly belated: Phillis felt the same; they gloomingly looked each other in the face from a distance, and maintained their distance so long as they could do so, for each feared one would communicate evil to the other.

This was an hour of intense anxiety; for here were Washington himself and Miss Nelly Custis, who were very apt to be walking round at dusk, and asking questions that might be difficult to answer. And there were also certain "loquacious damsels" employed about the mansion, who were much dreaded as spies on the conduct of the native Africans and their immediate descendants. Dolly first began to shorten the distance between her and Aunt Phillis, and determined to hear the worst if possible, approached the latter personage, with footsteps indicating the most decided want of elasticity. Coming near, at last, looking was abundant, but conversation scanty and evasive; for both feared that Thomas, the turkey driver, in search of new scenes of interest to his flock, had, this trip, ventured too far, and found, to his sorrow and undoing, certain scenes far too dangerously beautiful. Like the mariner lured to destruction by the melody of Siren voices on the Coast of Italy, they feared that the objects of their solicitude had drifted somewhere in the region of the "snare of the fowler," or the haunts of the unconquerable black fox. Thus they stood till grey twilight began to darken swiftly into sable night, and the shrill notes of the "Caty-Did," answering back to the "Caty-Did-Not," began to render night hideous to the ears on which sounds of sorrow had so recently fallen. To make things still more doleful, old Vulcan, the ancient historic hound, disturbed, perhaps, by the melancholy stillness of departing day and advancing night, opened up from the kennel, and began to howl in prolonged strains of the most doleful E flat. Phillis and Dolly sank deeper and deeper into the surging ocean of trouble; but their eyes keenly sought, in the dimness of twilight, the narrow paths winding over the sombre hills, and fondly but fearfully dwelt upon the sight. Dire phantoms, multiform and fleet-footed, haunted their being; and the sweetest notes of the grating knitting needle in still summer eve, or the most sprightly notes of the sprightliest "Caty-Did," would now have grated discordantly upon the tender nerves of the soul. The historic hound continued to howl and send up with renewed energy his deep-toned wailings, until the two old ladies, beside themselves with dread, by simultaneous thought and action, cast off their shoes, spit into them, and turned them bottom upwards on the ground, to break the *spell*, avert the threatened calamity, and silence the howling of the hound.

They trembled, and huge drops of perspiration started from the brow, for fear that Washington, the "white ladies," or some "loquacious damsel" serving at the mansion, might come out, ask questions, and discover the want of tone at the poultry-yard and in certain other localities. The weightiest considerations were suspended on the events of that hour. Old Vulcan had almost ceased to howl; the shoes, having performed their task of duty, found their respective feet again—but, O stars! what will Marse say? was the oft-repeated and unanswerable question. Washington is great, and good and kind, thought they; and yet, by some want of caution, his interests are about to suffer; for the kind and careful words of the turkey driver's commission have probably been forgotten or disregarded. They now looked through falling tears only for the sunshine of hope; but O, what horror mingled with hope, shifted the scene, as Thomas sprang over the kitchen-garden fence, and stood before them, *like a spectre, haggard, speechless and turkeyless !*

Aunt Phillis seized him and rudely hauled him into her cottage; Aunt Dolly followed, and, at the same moment, old Tige, the watch-hound, rushed up against the suddenly closed door, and uttered two or three yells of the most decided character.

Dolly soon learned that the whole flock of turkeys had been lost, and not been seen by their driver since twelve or one o'clock. She

hurried away and quickly closed the door of the turkey house, that
it might *appear* that the flock was all in and safely gone to roost,
should any person come "spyin' round" in that direction. On her
way back to Phillis's cottage, she saw Washington come round from
the eastern portico of the mansion, where he was walking, and look
up and down the roads leading to the entrance gates. Perhaps the
unseasonable yells of his favorite old hound brought him out to
see if some stranger was approaching the gates; but, discovering
nothing unusual, and nothing "out of *tune*," he soon returned to his
family group on the pavement. In all his eventful "peregrinations
through life," it is not likely that Washington was ever so unwel-
come a visitor at any place, as when he visited the western front of
his mansion on that evening.

"Lor ! Marse might ax me sumpin', and den what ?" mused Aunt
Dolly, as she hastened from his presence toward the now unhappy
home of Aunt Phillis, and she passed also several servants tumbled
on the grass, whose presence at that particular time was not much
less objectionable to her than that of the chief a moment previous.

Phillis and Dolly, being native Africans, or their immediate descendants, were now in great perplexity, for fear some of the "Virginia niggers," or the "white ladies" at the mansion, might snuff the
wind, and smell a tangible *mice*, before they could summon their
counsellors and determine on some course of proceeding suited to
the emergency. Being a weighty matter, and no every day occur-
rence, it demanded an immediate summon for all the united wisdom
of the Mount, and matters, too, were somewhat critical on account
of a certain degree of jealousy that existed between the "Virginia
niggers" and the native Africans; for it was well known in *high
circles* that the former had "blowed" on the latter in certain times
of scrape and difficulty.

Billy, the old huntsman and body-servant of the chief, was a
"Virginia nigger,"(but he was faithful and trustworthy ; kind to all,
and drew no lines of distinction between the two classes. Phillis
and. Dolly, with poor little Thomas, the unlucky turkey driver,
were, therefore, soon moving with silent tread, under cover of night,
across the lawn in the direction of Billy's quarters, to lay the whole
matter before him ; a messenger was despatched to "Dogue Run"
and "Muddy Hole" plantations, with a summons for Scomberry and
Bristol, the philosophers resident there, and a spy sent into Wash-

ington's camp, to reconnoitre the movements of that great general and his forces. The spy aforesaid was no less a personage than Mose, the cow-boy, who was commissioned to know nothing "whatsomebber," should he be captured by any of the "white folks," "blowin' niggers," or "loquacious damsels."

The sharp cow-boy cheerfully entered upon his hazardous duty, full of interest and sympathy for his noble but unfortunate young peer ; deeply sorry in the meantime, that he had dropped over the garden fence in a condition so speechless and turkeyless ; and other trusty servants, possessed of the unpleasant secret, for fear of being interrogated before it was time, had made circuitous tracks for Billy's quarter, or departed for some part or parts unknown to vulgar gaze.

The spy soon returned, having penetrated Washington's camp to its very centre ; and, seated at the council fire of the great colored sachem of Mount Vernon, he announced his reconnoissance successful ; that Washington and the white ladies had "gone in," and all was quiet along the lines. The sage forms seated around the council fire of their chief rejoiced that no odor of mice had been snuffed, and that "the cat was still safely bagged," to be admitted to daylight, at such a time and in such a manner only, as the council now in extraordinary session might direct. Billy commanded that the cow-boy be seated, with "fly-trap" closed, until called upon to speak or act; and, having the whole affair at his disposal, he quickly sent out ambassadors from his court to summon to his aid such great men as he appeared to need on this important occasion. Aunt Betty, the cook, was the first "wise persin" summoned to Billy's headquarters. She was put in possession of certain facts, and detailed to take charge of certain "loquacious damsels" serving at the headquarters of Washington, and to see to making things so dull and *toneless* about her as to induce them to "go to bed" a little earlier than usual.

"Tom's been 'sperimentin' in long dribes, and lost de turkeys," said Mose, the messenger sent for Betty, whispering a little too loud. It happened that Myrtilla, one of these damsels aforesaid, was present when Mose whispered to Betty, and strained her ears to catch the words, and would have caught them, had not Old Vulcan, ever present for good or evil, plunged his head into a pan of pot liquor, and loudly lapped away at the liquid with his long tongue.

Betty, Dolly and Phillis were rivals in plantation philosophy and domestic economy, delighting in "hooks" upon each other ; but all three came together as one in this great trial—great trial, we say—because it was a dark night, with sky overcast with most threatening clouds, and more than one hundred turkeys, the pride of the poultry yard and dining table at Mount Vernon, all lost, and their whereabouts even beyond the pale of rational conjecture. Aunt Phillis generally "outgeneralled" her rivals in both wit and policy, but the poor old lady had nothing to boast of this time; for she certainly had the deeper anxiety of the three, on account of her child's terrible misfortune.

All this time Thomas was closely confined in a close corner of the room—with grave philosophers towering above him, ever and anon covering him with the shadows cast from their dark forms—tearfully reflecting on his sad condition, as well as that of his lost flock, until he was called upon to give an account of his disastrous adventure. Aunt Dolly was cautiously moving round to guard all avenues to the secret, or give the wink to certain trusty servants that something dreadful was "afoot" at Mount Vernon, and that the presence of all the "knowin' persons" inhabiting the Mount was in immediate demand at the headquarters of the venerable body-servant.

Early in the night, several wise heads visiting from adjacent plantations began to assemble at different quarters, as company or inclination directed, to spend the evening in conversation, mirth and song ; but it was soon discovered that a dead weight, a singular inertia, was pressing somewhere ; that something was decidedly "afoot," for the looks of each seemed to indicate to the other that some strange mystery hung over the boundless freedom and generosity of the Mount. Scomberry and Bristol, the famous sages of Dogue Run and Muddy Hole, arrived at the "Home Plantation" just in time to break a dark cloud that began to rise in Aunt Phillis's sky for fear something had occurred to prevent their attendance ; and they were directed to hasten to Billy's council fire, where they were soon made acquainted with the outlines of the great problem to be then and there solved. It was now more than nine o'clock ; the night dark and cloudy, and premonitory of wind, rain and thunder ; but in the face of the warring elements, a number of the wise heads, both male and female, had assembled in council.

Thomas was now called up from his corner to face the assembled wisdom of the Mount, make his defence, and show cause, if any he had, why his command had been forsaken, squandered, or captured by the enemy.

"I driv my *tarkeys* way down 'long siden de ribber," said he, with tears chasing each other down his care-worn face; "I sot down to watch 'em, and soon drapped fas' asleep, and when I woke up my *tarkeys all done gone !*"

"Dar," exclaimed Aunt Phillis, throwing up her hands, and wildly rolling her eyes, "I *tole you sumpin' hit me on de nose: I tole you sumpin' gwine to happen.*"

A profound silence ensued. "I breaks de silence," said Sambo, the cobbler of the Mount; "and am ob de 'pinion you better be makin' de longest kind o' strides arter de tarkeys."

The cobbler would talk when his conversation was irrelevant and foolish ; and to hear him in a strain learnedly dwelling upon the mysteries of his art, you might conclude that he

> "Could shoe a gnat, or shave a fly ;
> Could nimbly cut mosquitoes' corns ;
> Or pare their nails, or sharp their horns."

Without much ado, the council appointed a committee, consisting of Cully, Sr., Cully, Jr , Mose, the cow-boy, Thomas, the schoolmaster, and several lesser lights, to proceed forthwith in search of the turkeys, though it was strongly urged that an attempt to force them from their roost and drive them home on such a dark night, might result in greater loss than to risk them out till daybreak.

Cully, Sr., being chairman, and Thomas, the driver, added to the committee as guide, they departed to wander about in the thick underbrush of the woods, and thicker darkness, in search of the lost flock. Bewildered and distressed in mind, poor little Thomas endeavored, as best he could, to pilot the committee to the spot where he slept, and where the turkeys deserted him, and swiftly moved along by different roads and serpentine paths, until he suddenly halted in a dark thicket, about one mile from the council house of the Sachem.

"Dis isent de right way," said Thomas. "It's too dark to find de tarkeys 'fore moon up ;" and the committee sat down in the deep darkness, under a thick spreading tree, to "study up sumpin," and to take council of each other as to what might be done under the circumstances. After a few moments of hasty conversation, in which all took some part, Cully, the chairman, cast about in the dark for some wandering ray of light, and concluded that the thick darkness on earth, and the frowning clouds in the heavens, were indeed frightful, and that no turkey could be found that night, unless, by accident, he might stumble on a *dead one.* This thought gave him the horrible idea of dead turkeys; and whilst indulging in gloomy thoughts of the darkness, and the probable fate of the flock, he imagined he saw, with eyes of flesh, the walking phantoms of the dead flock, marching through the thicket with measured step to the music of dry and rattling bones! Cully, therefore, soon gave evidence that he was disturbed by some terrible apparition; bewildered in mind, incoherent in speech, and unwilling to proceed. He felt that every turkey was surely dead; that some untracked carnivorous "varmint," unknown to the philosophy of the age, had swallowed down the entire flock at a mouthful.

"I sees wid dese eyes o' flesh o' mine," said he, gazing wildly into the dark thicket, "de ghoses ob de whole flock."

"I does, too, 'zackly," said the schoolmaster, rolling the white of his eye, and rising to prepare for evil. Fear had seized the learned pedagogue, and began to run like electric fire through his whole body, to the instantaneous quickening of his intellect. He put himself into the orator's posture, and began to address the terror-stricken committee; but thought was broken and language lame.

"Conscript Fathers!" said he, nervously lifting his hat from his fevered head, "I does not rise to waste de night in words. Let dat plebian talk—it's not my trade. I stands here for right—Roman right, sar; but none dare stand to take dar share wid me!"

He did not waste much time in words, but, advancing a little in front of the ghost-ridden committee, with face toward Mount Vernon, he thought many terrible thoughts; but, at last, determined to continue his speech to the regiment of ghosts before him.

"Ye 'lusive forms!" said he, "ye wild fantastic images, what is ye? Perhaps 'tis fancy all; and yet my eyes will seek dat fatal spot, and fondly dwell upon the sight what blasts 'em."

He paused to run, but could see no road out of the thicket; and he feared to run, had a road been there. Staring into the darkness before him, with eyes resting on the imaginary battalion of veritable ghosts, and body leaning forward, he continued his speech *a la Shakespeare*:

"Am dat a tarkey what I sees before me? Wid head toward my hand. Come, let me ketch thee. I has thee not; and yet I sees thee still. Is ye not, most awful wishun, sensible to feelin', as to sight. Or, is ye but a tarkey ob do mind—a false creation 'ceedin' from dis heated brain o' mine?"—and cutting his speech short, he "took to his heels," darting through the thicket toward Mount Vernon; the others following close in his rear,

"While yelling grisly shapes of dread
Came hunting on behind."

Poor little Thomas's bare feet played swiftly over the ground; but he kept close at the heels of the fugitive committee, until all reached the stable of the "home plantation" in safety, where they threw themselves on the grass to blow, and "study up" a report.

"What kind o' fathers am de conscript fathers?" inquired the cow-boy, rising from the grass and resting on his knees before the committee.

"Humphf!" said the schoolmaster; "you 'spose I can see how to 'spound de Shakespeare to cow-dribers in de dark?"

The committee hastily agreed upon a report in accordance with the suggestion of little Thomas: that it was too dark to find the flock before moon up; and proceeded to deliver it at headquarters; but, by mutual agreement, nothing was to be "let on" about the procession of ghosts, nor the schoolmaster's speeches in the wilderness.

Soon after ten o'clock, they knocked at the door of the council-house for admittance: delivered their report, and recommended that all search be suspended until moon-up.

"Dar!" said Aunt Phillis, "I tole you sumpin gwine to happen."

"Keep dark," said Billy; "the turkeys are all safe up the trees."

"How de young tarkeys gwine to fly up trees?' inquired she.

Billy hesitated to answer, and glanced at Scomberry. "How de young tarkeys fly up de trees?" interrupted Scomberry, the philosopher of Dogue Run. I soon 'monstrate dis to you. I has scraped de 'bacca hill, as you well knows, under all 'maginable sarcumstances. One-fird o' de groun' 'sisted ob big flint stones ; one-fird o' little ones; one-fird o' roots and snags, and tudder fird 'sisted o' dirt ; so, you sees, I has scraped de hills when free-firds ob de 'ponent parts ob de 'foresed hills was 'tagonistic to de life ob de plant, and but one-fird 'dapted to its groff. Arter scrapin' de hills under de 'foresed 'couragin' sarcumstances, I'se sot out de plant, and stood de constant sentinel by it until de muncy hab chinked in Marse's pocket. 1 has, darfore, 'corded in dis 'normous brain o' mine all de larnin ob dis famous plant, and all de 'stinctions of de varmints, bofe small and great, dat spy round to chaw it. As de wisdom ob a nation 'pends on de quality ob de people's food, so 'pends also de sharpness ob de 'stinctions ob de insec's what feed on de 'bacca itself, or 'pon other insec's what *have* chawed it. Eb'ry man in dis 'lightened 'sembly knows dis am been a fac' in all ages ob de world, ever since Killes drug Hector *clean round de walls o' Troy*. All dis, howsomeber, 'pends on de season when de eatin' am done—dat is, 'fore, arter, or in de time o' dog-days. You all well knows dat de great pest ob de 'bacca plant am de worm, as you can better know by lookin' at my *patch* jes at dis season. Dis 'structive insec' is hatched on de leaf o' de plant so fast dat you can see de process by de spyglass; and in a few days it comes ob age, when de sharp 'stinctions ob de young insec' leads it to dig a hole in de ground, about a feet or so deep, and *tomb* itself for a season. Dis has always been de habit ob de worm *eber sence Cadmus sot up school in de Greece*.

"Dis worm is de nat'ral production ob de plant. In dis self-made tomb, de insec' undergoes a bery 'laborate process o' 'morphosis, and soon 'pears again 'bove ground in de shape ob a sort o' butterfly, 'nominated by de planters de *horn-blower*, or he what blows a horn. De fust horn-blowers ob de season am hatched from other plants, as well as de 'bacca, and 'pear buzzin' and horn-blowin' 'mong de plants 'bout the fust o' June. But de horn-blower hatched from de 'culiar nature ob de 'bacca plant am de most 'stinctive and 'veterate ob all horn-blowers. Dis fust kind ob horn-blower dat comes in June is only actin' *possum*, and 'tendin' to hab a taste for de fine arts ob natur', by buzzin' round 'mong de flowers ; but he lies jes like de ole Lucifer; and de fust 'bacca plant dat peeps two inches outen de ground, he spies round arter it to 'posite de eggs o' destruction. Now, de worms produced from de horn-blower ob de month o' June, bab no 'ticular quality to nourish de body or sharpen de 'stinctions ob de animals what eat 'em ; but de worm produced from de horn-blower, produced from de 'bacca plant itself, am a different kind o' worm, and de mos' 'cidedly different o' 'fects am produced on de animals what eat 'em. In a few days de worms am growed to a size almost as big as your finger, and done chawed a pound ob de nasty green 'bacca. Now, here am dese insec's by de tens o' thousands, eatin' away on de plant and on de hopes ob de planter ; and while eatin' and 'gestin' dar food da makes a great noise, so dat de tarkey am 'tracted to de spot by de sound. He eats a great number ob de worms ; and when his craw 'pears jes like it's gwine to bust, he sets right into killin' de worms and tossin' 'em on de ground, jes like he does it for spite, till de ground am most kivered wid de 'funcked carcasses. Dis am de greatest kind o' 'musement for de young tarkeys, and da soon comes mos' 'normous fond ob de sport. Each season dar am *two gluts o' worms*, 'nominated de *fust* and *second glut*, and dis has bin de case eber sense de 'Postle Paul *went sailin' up and down in the 'pelago ob Greece, and 'sputin' wid de King o' 'Grippa.*

De second glut am always bound to be on hand in de dog-days, jes at dis time o' year ; and if you's mind to go down to my patch, I'll pint out to de wisdom ob dis 'liberative body de 'culiar worm ob de second glut, dat 'parts wisdom to de tarkey what eats 'em. As soon, darfore, as a tarkey gets his supper on de second glut o' worms provided de dog-days are gwine on at de same time, dat same tarkey am made *wise* by de flavor ob de worms—his wings 'come strong and ready to fly ; and soon as a varmint comes spyin' round, he takes to his heels and flies right up a tree. You all know, darfore, dat all de tarkeys, bofe old and young, hab tasted de second glut in dog-days ; and it is manifest to dis 'gust body o' liberators, dat when a varmint come arter de flock o' tarkeys, da all gwine to fly up trees."

What happened in the further deliberations of the council during the whole night—in the discovery and bringing home of the flock next morning, long after sunrise—in the trial of delinquents before Washington, and in the application of the subject by Scomberry, will fill a volume for the future. Suffice it to say, that the flock was recovered with the loss of *four* only of its members.

In Scomberry's third speech before the assembled wisdom of Mount Vernon, on the subject of the loss of the turkeys, he recited a poem—for he was a poet as well as a philosopher—and we quote as follows:

"I'se gwine to 'ply de auger as in de days ob ole,
And froo de mighty future I'se gwine to bore a hole;
An ax ole Time to 'form me how things am gwine to stand,
In all de mighty future o' 'Lumbia's happy land.
I'se gwine to 'larm de sleepers dat swarm de shores o' time,
And wake up ebry nigger dis side o' Afric's clime;
I'se gwine to show de sleepers dat snore late in de morn,
Jes how da's bin a snorin', *wid tarkeys all done gone.*

"I went to Alexandria quite late one arternoon,
And counted on returnin' jes 'fore de set o' moon;
I stepped into de tabern jes arter candle-light,
Jes like I gwine to ax 'em for lodgin' for de night;
One fellow say, here, nigger, come, take a glass o' rum,
For why you stand dar gazin' jes like you's deaf and dumb?
I stepped up to de counter—dere sot a bottle full—
I did not 'pear much bashful, but took a 'normous pull;
I soon felt right for chattin' and wid de men sot down;
Who said, we's from de army dat's close to Bostin town;
We's agents for de lottery ob dese United States,
And peddles round de tickets at 'commodatin' rates.
I jes pulled out my money, but wasn't gwine to buy;
But offered half a dollar, my fortin jes to try;
Says he, I specs you's groggy—O, dat's not gwine to do:
You must be 'normous skittish, or stingy like a Jew:
Jes hand me dat *five dollars* you's holdin' in dat paw,
And here's de lucky ticket what will *ten thousand* draw.
I handed him de money jes for de fear o' scorn,
And jumped right up next mornin, wid *tarkeys all done gone.*
Whene'er I sees men blowin' jes about dar putty face,
And braggin' 'bout dar runnin' ob de gymnasty race;
Dar gwine to be 'cumsissled and lose as sure's you born,
And wake up late some mornin', *wid tarkeys all done gone.*

\n if he 'gins to snore at night widout fust lookin' round,
To lock his hen and meat house, and let loose ebry hound,
Nex mornin' he'll come spyin' round wid basket full o' corn,
But drap de basket, cryin',' *my tarkeys all done gone.*
And robbers ob de hen roost what spy all round o' nights,
Am bound to spy de sheriff, and see some shockin' sights ;
And march down to de jail house, quite early in de morn,
Look froo de iron windows *wid tarkeys all done gone.*

"I pauses here to 'mind you ob poor old Cesar Corn,
Who was, wid one exception, de best old nigger born,
I'll tell you dat exception, a few words am de sum,
He went to Fairfax court house, and died o' drinkin' rum.
One day young Cesar, junior, his only lubly son,
Rode down to town a horse-back to hab a little fun,
He went into the tabern, called for a quart o' rum,
De landlord said, you's hard, sar, jes like a stump o' gum ;
But out he fotch de liquor, jes in a quart tin cup—
And said, you aint, sar, is you, now gwine to drink dat up ?
Young Cesar, like a sabbage, his hat tossed on de floor,
Dat's jes what killed my father, said he, and made him poor,
Ise bound to hab revenge, sar, jes 'fore I leaves dis town,
And grabbin' at de quart cup, de rum he swallowed down.
Den right home in a gallop went junior Cesar Corn,
But waked up *dead* nex mornin' *wid tarkeys all done gone.*

"A fop jes goes out sparkin' wid hair all round his mouf,
And passes 'mong de ladies, a planter from de Souf ;
O my ! says one, he's charmin,' he's lubly, and he's rich ;
I'll jes fro down dis sewin,' widout another stitch,
And polish up my beauty, and to de party go ;
I'll gib dis world, for sartin, to catch a wealthy beau,
I lubs dat smoove muffstasher, dat rollin' sparklin' eye,
And what is more de beauty, he moves in circles high.
She locks her arm in hisen, and gaily trots along,
Jes happy as de huntsman, what sings de huntsman's song.
But soon she wakes some mornin' all covered o'er wid smut,
And wise as de young tarkey what eat de *second glut.*

5

"I holds a sheet o' paper jes 'fore dis candle light,
 You sees it widout blemish, so stainless, pure and white,
 Jes tech it to dat candle, or black it gin dat pot,
 Or take dat pen up yonder, and on it make a blot,
 Den you can rub and rub it, or scrape it wid your knife,
 But you aint gwine to 'rase it, or clean it, save your life.
 But you may keep on rubbin,' and scrapin' till you's riled,
 But neber can restore it—de sheet o' paper's spiled,
 And worthless for de writer, and worse for printin' on,
 And frow'd among de rubbish, jes till its old and gone.
 I warns dat fair young lady, what 'herits a fair name,
 To sharply watch her actions for fear she'll sile her fame,
 For if her fair character should eber get a stain,
 Jes like dat sheet 'o paper, it can't come white again,
 But frow'd back 'mongst de rubbish her foolishness to mourn,
 She'll wake up ebry mornin' *wid tarkeys all done gone.*

"Now when you sees a people rebellin' gin all rule,
 And 'spoundin' constitutions, and kickin' like de mule,
 Den on 'em come de ruin, destruction fierce and sad,—
 Jes 'fore de gods destroy us da gwine to make us mad,
 And all de politicians are gwine to bump dar head,
 And up will rise de people, and kill false leaders dead,
 And hurl 'em down from power to livin' in a hut,
 As wise as half-grown tarkeys what eat *de second glut.*
 De persons dats 'bovementioned who try to be so great,
 And 'tempt a rebolution, and seize de cheer ob state,
 Will wake at eve, I augers, or very late next morn,
 And cry, by de ole Jupiter! *my tarkeys all done gone.*

"Jes see dat red nose tippler, ob 'ciety de scum,
 Dat has no brains outsiden his little jug o' rum,
 Now—*hiccup*—says he—*hiccup*—dis country's gone 'stray,
 De wise men ob dis nation am all done lost de way.
 Now—*hiccup*—come here—*hiccup*—come take jes one more dram,
 Dis—*hiccup*—constitution am all a—*hiccup*—sham.
 Ise for a constitution dat's—hiccup—just and strong,
 I finds de 'mortal sages ob eighty-seven wrong.

Now down to town comes ridin' de haughty demagogue,
And says to hisself, musin,' "dat fool am full o' grog.
"But free-fourths ob de voters am like dat drunken shoat,
"And yet dis constitution allows sich trash to vote,
"His jug o' rum cost sixpence, his coat 'bout half a crown,
"We'll set the poor fools fitin' and pull dar wages down;
"I owns a thousand acres and 'bout a hundred slaves,
"And yet I has but one vote jes like dese drunken knaves
"Dat's bound to get in office and make dis nation's laws,
"Den we rich, proud old *rusty* crats must shake dar dirty paws.
"I swears by de ole Jupiter, dis business neber do,
"For by dis constitution the poor might get rich too.
"We'll start a war for *freedom*, and at the flag will scoff,
"And under dis pretention we'll kill the poor trash off."
But traitors neber flourish in 'Lumbia's happy land,
But treason's gwine to perish by its own bloody hand,
And stumble gin de saw log and be in sunder sawn,
Or tumble o'er de mill-dam, *wid tarkeys all done gone.*

CHAPTER IV.

HAVING noticed the turkey story of '97, and its morals, we come to the New Year of '98. A happy Christmas had been spent at the mansion and at the servants' quarters; but the festivities of the season had not been passed without adding here and there a new song to beautify and cheer the Mount.

But six months have passed away since the choirs last met in open air in '97. The flowers of May, '98, appear in bloom; and the poet of Dogue Run, profound in deliberation and classic in motion, appears again costumed as gaily as May herself. With cocked hat, short continental breeches, long stockings, low shoes with silver buckles, and long blue coat, he appeared on Whit-Monday, at the home plantation, flourishing a long tasseled wand, and with philosophic tread, found his way to Billy's cottage, mid a host of admirers. His appearance in full costume was the signal for the opening of the musical campaign of '98. He had recently spent much time beside his pure Castilian fountain, located less than half a stadium from his Delphian abode, diligently courting the Muses of the little Parnassus that towered above him; and, like an oracular priest on the tripod, tarrying for a response, his flowing white locks made venerable the secluded shades of Green Willow Hollow.

In the early part of the year 1798, a certain discovery was made to improve the provincial *corn-cob pipe.* The collector of the port of Mount Vernon claimed the honor of the discovery. He was a wily old contrabandist, and generally received the duties on imports in Jamaica rum. This quickened his powers of invention, kept alive the fire in his pipe, and caused him to set in grave analysis of the corn-cob. He therefore discovered that pipes must be made of cobs plucked from the field and shelled in a certain *season*. In honor of the discovery and its author, the poet of Green Willow Hollow consented to court the Muses of his little Parnassus; and on the beautiful Whit-Monday of '98, after those famous pipes had undergone the test of six months' trial, the groves of Mount Vernon were made vocal for the first time of the season, and the corn-cob pipe seized the immortality of song. On the green grass, between the summer-house and old vault, and within hearing of the chief and white ladies of the mansion, the choir sang as follows:

O how sweet de breeze am blowin',
    Now de heat ob day am past;
And how bright de stars am glowin,
    Since de clouds hab floated past.

From dat pole de banners' streamin',
    Feelins in dis breast it 'spires;
But while all dis beauty's beamin',
    I my corn-cob pipe admires.

Let de statesman climb de mountain
    Arter glory's giddy seat;
Let de scholar sip de fountain,
    Let him call de *hard-books* sweet.

Let de maiden 'dulge her dreamin',
    'Bout de future days o' bliss;
Let de rose in twilight gleamin,
    Meet de jessamine and kiss.

Smokers babble 'bout out-smokin'
    'Lympus Jupiter ob old;
But I tells you widout jokin,'
    'Bout dis pipe de haf's not told.

Now we hears the hard-hooks croakin,'
    "Jupiter de nectar sips;"
But de books can't tell how smokin'
    'Parts de flavor to de lips.

In dis pipe de fire am glowin,'
  See dat smoke!—it curls and turns ;
  See it fanned by breezes blowin'!
  As I sucks it, how it burns.

From de cob jes *in de season*
  Wid dis hand I shelled de corn ;
  De time o' shellin' am de reason,
  Why its sweet and hard like horn.

CHORUS.—Now I guesses you confesses,
  Sweet must be dis 'brosial smoke,
  For I'se jokin' while I'se smokin'
  Dis mos charmin' corn-cob pipe.

In this year, Thomas, the unsuccessful turkey driver of '97, appeared in light continental breeches, long white stockings, low shoes with buckles, long white apron and powdered hair, standing at the table of the mansion, as an assistant in the dining room. How changed he is! He has grown much taller, and his well-formed ebony face is always lit up with the most pleasing smiles. Lady Washington and Miss Nelly admire and praise him, and express their pleasure that a youth so clean, so active, and so smiling, has been found on the Mount Vernon estate. His qualifications demand his services at the mansion, and he has been ordered into Frank's department as an assistant dining-room servant. In preparing the dining table, he would hold in his right hand a dish, a plate of butter, or water glass, and with his keen eye fixed on Frank, his superior, would flourish it over his head without dropping its contents, and let it "come to time" with Frank, holding a similar vessel, so as to produce but one sound as if but one vessel only had touched the table at the moment of contact. This pleased his superior, and in order to give his young assistant practice in the art, two glasses were filled to the brim with water, Frank taking one and Thomas the other, and flourishing them clearly over their heads would bring them to time on the table without spilling a drop of water.

But during those sweet dreams of peace the French war cloud, before referred to, began to gather in earnest. "Preparations were made for war with France, and in May, '98, Congress authorized the formation of a large military force to be called a provisional army. The movement was popular with the people, and with anxious hearts, their thoughts turned instinctively to Washington, as their commander-in-chief."

"I must tax you sometimes for advice," writes President Adams to the retired chief at Mount Vernon. "We must have your *name*, if you will in any case permit us to use it. There will be more efficiency in it than in many an army."

"You see how the storm thickens," wrote the Secretary of War, "and that our vessel will soon require our ancient pilot. Will you— may we flatter ourselves that, in a crisis so awful and important— you will accept the command of all our armies? I hope you will, because you alone can unite all hearts and all hands, if it is possible they can be united."

"I see, as you do," writes Washington, to the Secretary of War, "that clouds are gathering, and that a storm may ensue, and I find, too, from a variety of hints, that my quiet under these circumstances, does not promise to be of long continuance."

"And now there were stirring times again at Mount Vernon. Washington's post-bag came filled with a score of letters sometimes, for to him had been entrusted the selection of officers for the army, and there were thousands of aspirants for places of almost every grade."

President Adams had already nominated to the Senate, "George Washington, of Mount Vernon, to be Lieutenant-General and Commander-in-Chief of all the armies raised and to be raised in the United States."

The patriotism of the country was once more stirred from centre to circumference, if any it had—for the centre of liberty appeared *every where*—but its circumference *no where*—the war clarion awakened all those patriotic feelings which local associations are calculated to awaken, and grounds which had been dignified by wisdom, bravery and virtue, in former days, caused every man's patriotism to revive and "gain force."

"On the 19th December, 1776, when the stoutest hearts failed," Thomas Paine, that accomplished American political writer, "published his first 'Crisis,' which began with that phrase since so often quoted: *'These are the times that try men's souls.'* This aroused the drooping ardor of the people; it was read at the head of every regiment; and the first fruit of the re-animated enthusiasm it produced was the battle of Trenton, six days after."

In '98, Paine's words, uttered when British tyranny was about to be hurled from power on this continent, were still fresh in the memory of many a war-worn patriot of '76, and now the days that tried men's souls were at hand again, for the haughty French Directory must be humbled, and the insult offered the United States must be wiped out in blood, unless some delicate diplomacy can adjust the difficulty.

New York, ever at her post of honor in *all* hours of the nation's trouble, was first on the stage to play her part in the bloody drama of '98, if the worst must come. She roused her sons to duty, rallied to the national standard, and sung the first war song of the day, called

"THE FEDERAL CONSTITUTION BOYS, AND LIBERTY FOREVER."

"Poets may sing of their Helicon streams,
  Their gods and their heroes are fabulous dreams,
          They ne'er sang a line
          Half so grand, so divine,
          As the glorious toast
          We Columbians boast,
  The *Federal Constitution* boys, and *Liberty* forever.

"ADAMS, *the man of our choice*, guides the helm,
  No tempest can harm us, no storm overwhelm,
          Our sheet anchor's sure,
          And our bark rides secure,
          So here's to the toast
          We Columbians boast,
  The *Federal Constitution* boys, and the *President* forever.

"A free navigation, commerce and trade,
  We'll seek for no foe, of no foe be afraid;
          Our frigates shall ride
          Our defence and our pride;
          Our tars guide our coast
          And huzza for our toast,
  The *Federal Constitution*, *Commerce* and *Trade forever*.

"Montgomery and Warren still live in our songs;
Like them our young heroes shall spurn at our wrongs,
    The world shall admire,
    The zeal and the fire,
    Which blaze in the toast
    We Columbians boast,
The *Federal Constitution*, and its *advocates* forever.

"When an enemy threats all party shall cease;
We *bribe* no intruders to buy a mean peace;
    Columbians will scorn,
    Friends or foes to suborn,
    We'll ne'er stain the toast,
    Which as freemen we boast,
The *Federal Constitution*, and *Integrity* forever.

"Fame's trumpet shall swell in Washington's praise,
And *Time* grant a furlough to lengthen his days;
    May health weave the thread
    Of delight round his head—
    No nation can boast
    Such a man—such a toast—
The *Federal Constitution* boys, and Washington forever."

In those days of pure and undivided patriotism, there "could not be gotten together any large public assembly without a considerable spice of the Revolution being among it. The soldiers and sailors of the war for liberty abounded in all public places, and no sooner would their old chief appear, than off came each hat, and the shout of welcome resounded, pure, spontaneous—direct from the heart."

A piece of music, set for the harpsichord, entitled the "President's March," was composed in 1789, by a German named Fayles, on the occasion of Washington's *first* visit to a theatre in New York.

"When it was announced that President Washington would attend, the theatres of that day would be crowded from top to bottom, as many to see the hero as the play. Upon the President's entering the stage-box with his family, the orchestra would strike up the 'President's March,' and the audience would applaud. This March was generally called for by the deafening din of an hundred voices at once, and upon its being played, three hearty cheers would rock the building to its base."

But from behind the war-cloud of '98, which obscured the happy land of Washington, arose the bright star of

"HAIL COLUMBIA,"

and took its place in the canopy of nations.

As the stars have ever been "the points where all that ever lived have met, the great, the small, the evil and the good; the prince, the warrior, the statesman, sage; and as every man that has looked up from the earth to the firmament has met every other man among the stars, for all have seen them alike," even so shall all men—progenitors, cotemporaries, and posterity, in the land consecrated by the footprints of Washington—meet at "Hail Columbia," and bless that bright star which first found its orbit in 1798.

In this year, Joseph Hopkinson, son of Francis Hopkinson, Esq., a signer of the Declaration of Independence, wrote "Hail Columbia," in Philadelphia, for a young actor there, named Fox. Mr. Hopkinson was then a rising young lawyer, of twenty-eight years of age. "At that time war with France was expected, and a patriotic feeling pervaded the community. Mr. Fox, a young singer and actor, called upon Mr. Hopkinson one morning, and said, "To-morrow evening is appointed for my benefit at the theatre. Not a single box has been taken, and I fear there will be a thin house. If you will write me some patriotic verses to the tune of the President's March, I feel sure of a full house. Several people about the theatre have attempted it, but they have come to the conclusion it cannot be done, yet I think you may succeed."

Mr. Hopkinson retired to his study, wrote the first verse and chorus, and submitted them to Mrs. Hopkinson, who sang them to a harpsichord accompaniment. The tune and the words harmonized. The song was soon finished, and that evening the young actor received it. We copy from an edition which appeared in the spring of '99.

> Hail Columbia! happy land,
> Hail ye heroes, heaven-born band,
>   Who fought and bled in Freedom's cause,
>   Who fought and bled in Freedom's cause,

And when the storm of war was gone,
Enjoyed the peace your valor won,
Let Independence be your boast,
Ever mindful what it cost;
Ever grateful for the prize,
Let its altar reach the skies—
    Firm—united let us be,
    Rallying round our Liberty,
    As a band of brothers joined,
    Peace and safety we shall find.

Immortal Patriots! rise once more,
Defend your rights—defend your shore;
Let no rude foe with impious hand,
Let no rude foe with impious hand,
Invade the shrine where sacred lies,
Of toil and blood, the well-earned prize,
While offering peace, sincere and just,
In heaven we place a manly trust,
That truth and justice will prevail,
And every scheme of bondage fail—
    Firm—united let us be,
    Rallying round our Liberty,
    As a band of brothers joined,
    Peace and safety we shall find.

Sound, sound, the trump of fame,
Let Wasnington's great name
Ring through the world with loud applause,
Ring through the world with loud applause,
Let every clime to Freedom dear,
Listen with a joyful ear—
With equal skill, with God-like power,
He governs in the fearful hour
Of horrid war, or guides with ease,
The happier times of honest peace.
    Firm—united let us be,
    Rallying round our Liberty,
    As a band of brothers joined,
    Peace and safety we shall find.

Behold the chief who now commands,
Once more to serve his country stands
　　The rock on which the storm will beat,
　　The rock on which the storm will beat,
　　But armed in virtue, firm and true,
　　His hopes are fixed on heaven and you—
　　When hope was sinking in dismay,
　　When glooms obscured Columbia's day,
　　His steady mind from changes free,
　　Resolved on death or Liberty—
　　　　Firm—united let us be,
　　　　Rallying round our Liberty,
　　　　As a band of brothers joined,
　　　　Peace and safety we shall find."

"The next morning the theatre placards announced that Mr. Fox would sing a new patriotic song. The house was crowded, the song was sung, the audience was delighted, eight times it was called for, and repeated, and when sung the ninth time, the whole audience stood up and joined in the chorus. Night after night 'Hail Columbia' was applauded in the theatres; and in a few days it was the universal song of the boys in the street."

We have not seen that writers have fixed the precise time in '98, when Mr. Hopkinson penned "Hail Columbia." Good authority gives "the summer of 1798," but it must have dated back to a time quite early in that year, for Edward Livingston, in a speech in Congress on the "Alien Bill," the 21st of June, appears to quote it as follows—"Do not let us be told, sir, that we excite a fervor against foreign aggression only to establish tyranny at home; that like the arch-traitor, we cry 'Hail Columbia' at the moment we are betraying her to destruction; that we sing out 'happy land,' when we are plunging it to ruin and disgrace, and that we are absurd enough to call ourselves free and enlightened, while we advocate principles that would have disgraced the age of Gothic barbarity and established a code, compared with which the ordeal is wise, and the trial by battle is merciful and just."

But soon "the attitude assumed by the United States, and the appearance of Washington at the head of the army, humbled the

French Directory, and President Adams was encouraged to send
representatives to France again. When they arrived, towards the
close of 1799, the weak Directory were no more. Napoleon Bona-
parte was at the head of the government as First Consul, and soon
the cloud of war that hung between the United States and France,
was dissipated."

It was in November, 1781, soon after the memorable surrender of
Cornwallis at Yorktown, that a band of gentlemen and ladies, vocal
and instrumental musicians of great powers, assembled in the "Temple of Minerva," represented at the hotel of the Minister of France,
in Philadelphia. A stage was erected on which was personified the
"Genius of America," the "Genius of France," and the "High Priest
of Minerva."

In scene the first, the doors of the sanctuary being shut, the
genius of America first appeared and sang—

> "My warlike sons—the sons of fame,
>   In deeds of virtue bold;
> Among the nations humbly claim,
>   An honored place to hold."

The genius of France waved her bright wings, and replied—

> "Great Minerva, grant her prayer,
>   Make her valiant sons thy care;
> To the immortal breath of fame,
>   Give! O give! her honored name."

The high priest of Minerva, advancing in sacerdotal splendor,
sang in reply—

> "From the censer clouds ascending,
>   Hearts and voices sweetly blending;
> Shall to Minerva grateful prove,
>   And call down blessings from above."

Scene the second.—The doors of the sanctuary thrown open, and
the high priest advancing a little further, continued—

> "Behold the great daughter of Jove,
>   Behold, how resplendent in light!
> On a cloud she descends from above,
>   All glorious, revealed to the sight.

"Your songs have her favor obtained,
  She comes to reply to your prayer ;
And now what the fates have ordained,
  Minerva herself shall declare."

In the person of the most beautiful young lady of the Washingtonian age, the goddess suddenly moves forward in a dazzling glory, encircled with a rainbow of emerald, and sings—

"In the golden balance weighed,
  Have I seen Columbia's fate ;
All her griefs shall be repaid,
  By a future happy state ;
She, like the glorious sun,
Her resplendent course shall run—
  And future days
  Columbia's praise
Shall spread from east to west.
  The gods decree
  That she shall be
A nation great, confessed."

The genius of America then advanced and replied in triumphant song—

"Let earth's inhabitants, heaven's pleasure know,
And fame her loud uplifted trumpet blow ;
Let the celestial *nine* in tuneful choirs,
Touch their immortal harps with golden wires."

After one of the most magnificent banquets of melody the eighteenth century ever saw, in which some of the most glorious "prophecies in sound" were uttered, the three genii joined in the following friendly chorus, and closed the scene :

"Now the dreadful conflicts' o'er,
Now the cannons cease to roar ;
Spread the joyful tidings round,
Spread the joyful tidings round,
He comes, he comes, with conquest crowned.
  Hail Columbia's godlike son !
Hail the glorious Washington.

"Fill the golden *trump of fame*,
Through the world his worth proclaim,
Let rocks, and hills, and vales resound,
Let rocks, and hills, and vales resound,
He comes, he comes, with conquest crowned ;
    Hail Columbia's godlike son !
    Hail the glorious Washington."

The sweet tones of liberty uttered in the "Temple of Minerva" in '81, had not ceased to ring in the American heart in '89 ; but finding in '87, a record in the eternal flint of words, they swept along the banqueting places of earth down to the year of '98.

"Several people about the theatre have attempted it, but come to the conclusion it cannot be done," said Mr. Fox, when in '98 he desired some patriotic verses written to the tune of the President's March. But had not this task been almost accomplished in the preceding chorus, sung by the three genii, seventeen years before ?

Do not "Hail Columbia," the "trump of fame," and the measure of the chorus, appear to carry Fayles back from '89 to '81, for his music, and Hopkinson from '98 to the same scene, and the same year, for his words ? Who can say but our own immortal "Hail Columbia" had its real origin in the "Temple of Minerva," or in the surrender of Cornwallis, when "Magog among the nations" arose from his lair at Yorktown, and "shook, in the fury of his power, the insurgent world beneath him ?" May not Fayles have touched a key in the "Temple of Minerva" in '81, and revived the sound in '89 ? May not the eye of Hopkinson in '98 have fallen upon the "Columbian Parnassiad" of '87, when the "Temple of Minerva" first entered the great highway of history ? But none the less glory for Mr. Hopkinson.

If the war cloud of '98 brought no other refreshing shower to this thirsty earth, it cheered, refreshed and beautified the rising tree of liberty with "Hail Columbia." In the remote future of this happy land, when divisions and war shall rock our glorious form of free government, and our noble ship of state shall reel and stagger in the awful squall, Hail Columbia will live to let in the day-light of past ages on the scene. No battles will be successfully fought, no victories will be permanently won, without its thrilling melody and the glowing inspiration of its numbers.

Sounds which are but passing breath, being once uttered, may never cease to be repeated, and the universal song of the boys of '98, will be the song of the boys of unnumbered centuries to come. Other songs, like the owls and the bats, have fluttered for a season in the doubtful perspicuity of twilight, but Hail Columbia, like the eagle, has soared away to the sun.

There is not in existence a single line of verse by Chaldean, Babylonian or Phœnician bard, for

"They had no poet, and they died."

"They could embalm bodies, but hieroglyphics themselves failed to embalm ideas," but the bard of Philadelphia, by a few letters, as ships passing through the sea of time, has connected Hail Columbia with the remotest generations of the world. As, without song, the nations of the star-led magi, and the sun-worshipping Parsee, have died, even so, with Hail Columbia the free republic of Washington shall live! and because Washington still lives, Hail Columbia lives also, and will soar on wings of immortality, and gladden the nations of the earth till the last wave of history shall have been broken on the shores of time.

CHAPTER V.

It was "late peach time" in '98 before Hail Columbia was sung by the choir of Mount Vernon. Miss Nelly had gone through some hard practice of the new national song on the harpsichord; and every time she played and sang it, curious eyes and ears, both inside and outside the mansion, were turned to see and listen, and convey every sound and every word into the recesses of brains that knew no forgetfulness. In the latter part of the month, when the large white "October peaches" were fully ripe, and gathering time was at hand, a "peach party" assembled in and around the neat white cottage of Mr. and Mrs. Cully, Jr., to enjoy the first fruit of the late peach season, and sing Hail Columbia in honor of the chief who once again stood the rock on which the storm from the French war cloud must beat.

The best peaches that grew at the cottage doors of Mount Vernon on trees planted and reared by grey-haired servants long years gone by, were gathered and served in plates to the musical guests of the party then and there assembled. Sweet was the flavor of this delicious fruit, and frequent were the references to the pious memory of aged patriarchs of the Mount, now gone to rest, who planted the trees now yielding cheerful fruit for their children.

Large was the gathering under the spreading oaks before Cully Jr's door this evening, and cheerfully burned the large fire kindled in the grove to warm the chilling breezes of a night in autumn. Some grave thoughts however, intruded, for the last song of the "Caty-Did" was dying away in the distance, and the last serenade in

6ᶜ

open air for the season was now at hand. But Cully Jr's hospitality on this occasion knew no bounds, and never did the smoke from his rude wood and clay chimney, curl more hospitably; his vocabulary failed to furnish words sufficiently kind for the entertainment of his guests, and never was Myrtilla, once the "loquacious damsel," but now the refined, lady-like Mrs. Cully, Jr., more busy in preparing the grove for the accommodation of her guests. Seats of all kinds were in great demand—chairs, stools, and boards temporarily erected, were displayed over twenty square yards of the grove, and a conspicuous stand erected for "Little Jack" the leader, who was about to give his best "base, perpendicular, and hypotenuse" on Hail Columbia.

At this party appeared a very eccentric and witty negro, called "Fairfax Pompey," who was the slave of a merchant in Alexandria. He had recently been introduced into the society of Mount Vernon, and was quite a beau among the belles of the different plantations. His master bestowed upon him a large amount of the profits of his dray, which kept him in change, and enabled him to dress "out of sight" of the common people of his color, and ape the dandy with the most consummate skill and perfection. He had a good master, yet he did not like him too well, for the dandy was not a pro-slavery man, but thought all men were created free and equal, and that his master should therefore set him free.

At the peach party Pompey amused the company by the following anecdote of himself, which he told in all companies he visited, for years, before and after the present.

"What you spose I did las Sunday ?" inquired he.

"I gibs dat up," replied Peter, the superintendent of the stables. "What was it ?"

"I went up Huntin' Creek to Mefodis meetin'. "

"Well, what 'o dat, sar ?" inquired Peter.

"I jes sot down on a stone, dats' all," replied Pompey.

"You sot down on a stone !" exclaimed Peter. "What you do dat for ?"

"Nuffin 'tall, sar, but jes listen what de preacher gwine to say."

"Well, what did de preacher say ?"

"He say you cant sarve two marsers.'

"Well, what you think o' dat ?"

"I thought de preacher lied, sar, and jes took up dis hat and got off for home."

"Well, what nex' happened ?"

"Marse say, 'whar you bin Pompey?' "

"What you tell him, sar ?"

"I tole him I been to Mefodis preachin'."

"What he say den, sar ?"

"Been to preachin'!" said he, "Ise glad o' dat, Pompey. How you like de preacher, Pompey ?"

"What you answer, sar ?"

"Not a bit," sez I.

"What nex' ?"

"Why ?" sez he.

"What you answer ?"

"Kase he lies," sez I.

"What your masser say den ?"

"You rascal !" sez he, "how dare say a preacher lies ?"

"What you say den ?"

"Well, sar," sez I, "I'se jes gwine to show you how de preacher does lie. De preacher, sez I, said, 'you can't sarve two marsers, for you either love de one and hate de tudder, or cleave to de one and 'spise de tudder.' Now I does sarve two marsers—ole marse and young marse—dat's one lie, sez I, pullin' off my hat. Den he say, 'you love de one and hate de tudder'—dat's another lie, sez I—for de Lord knows I hates you bofe."

It was not before the time of the peach party of '98, that Christopher, the body-servant of the chief during the first and second terms of the Presidency at Philadelphia, ventured to tell his friends at Mount Vernon, what befel him and the first President of the United States, on their way from Philadelphia to Mount Vernon, in 1796.

Christopher's presence at the party was hailed as a harbinger of joy, for he was always ready to tell anecdotes and stories of what he had seen and heard among the great Fathers of the Republic, in Philadelphia. On this occasion, the guests of Cully Jr., at the peach party, gathered around Christopher, whose "large white eyes," and uncommonly black face, were lit up with smiles, and the most fascinating wit and humor played around his large and eloquent mouth. He proceeded to say, that, on a certain day in the fall of the year, he attended the first President of the United States on a journey through Kent county, in the State of Maryland—the journey being from Philadelphia to Mount Vernon—and they stopped at the house of an old soldier who had served under Washington at Germantown, Brandywine and Monmouth. When Washington's carriage came over the hill in sight of the old soldier's farm house, all eyes were turned towards it, and speculation was on tiptoe as to who the distinguished occupant could be. The carriage was drawn by two white horses and followed by a black man on horse-back. All this display was seen at a distance of about three-quarters of a mile, moving briskly along the road up to the farm house.

"Who can it be?" inquired one of the soldier's daughters, wringing her hands in wonder at the sight.

"Who can it be?" inquired another, throwing up her hands and raking down the person of a third.

"Who be dat?" shouted aunt Peggy, as she popped out of the kitchen, and ran across the yard.

"Hanged if I know," said the old soldier, straining his eye-balls at the sight.

"It must be de Gubner, wid coach and *tantum*," said aunt Peggy, with much confidence.

"I believe in my soul it's the King," said the mistress of farm house, clapping her hands and gazing down the highway.

General Washington, in journeying to and from the seat of government, had passed the old soldier's house several times in former years, and the family knew him well, but at this time none appeared to be thinking about the President. It was an unusual time of the year for him to be traveling, yet it is some matter of surprise that the sharp little daughters of the old soldier, who had seen him before, did not recognize him at this time. He had two little daughters aged respectively six and eight years, who were also standing with the rest of the family at the yard gate, and doing their best to discover the real facts in the case. Just as the whole group appeared to be speechless and absorbed in silent wonder, Lizzie, the younger of the two little girls, threw up her hands, and wildly rolling her eyes, sprang towards her mother, and shouted at the top of her voice, "Mother! Mother! it's General Washing*tub*."

"Good gracious!" exclaimed the old lady of the farm house, "he might come in," and off she flew towards the house, flourishing a formidable carving knife she held in her hand.

The grown daughters "took after her for life," and having reached the house, some ran up stairs, some into the kitchen, and others under the bed in the "big room," to put on "store clothes," to peep through the key hole, or lie under the bed and listen till he was gone.

The old soldier ran down the road to meet the carriage, his two little girls and four dogs ran after him ; and the colt alarmed by the sudden uproar, jumped "clean over the barn-yard fence and took across the corn-field for life." The carriage not being seen by them, the dogs, thinking the colt the offending object, jumped the fence, and striking his trail through the spreading corn that hid him from view, chased him round and round the field, sweeping, like the swift-winged hurricane, all the unfortunate corn-stalks before them.

When the old soldier, regardless of the destructive colt and dogs among his corn-stalks, met the carriage, the President reined up his horses, lit in the road, and heartily shook hands with his old companion in arms. Christopher dismounted—Washington took each of the little girls by the hand and led them to the house, the horses attached to the carriage were led by the postillion, and Christopher, the body-servant, leading his horse, followed along on foot. Thus organized, the procession soon reached the farm house, when, lo and behold! the colt and the dogs having bursted from the corn-field, leveling the fence before them, rushed madly along the road to their place of starting, where the colt leaped into the barn-yard, and the infuriated dogs halted to attack the carriage of the first President of the Republic.

A perfect picture of the great and the small, the sublime and the ridiculous, was fully exhibited, as the old soldier at the farm-house gate, sat before the horses of the President a "bite of corn," furnished in washing *tubs* from aunt Peggy's kitchen. The Chief stood by to see that all was right, and the horses well provided for; and then walked from the gate to the house, still leading the little girls, who appeared determined not to be slighted even by the President of the United States.

By this time the lady of the farm-house had slipped on a clean cap, swept up the dirt, removed the scraps from the table, and stood at the door ready to welcome her distinguished guest, but not until she had thumped the grown girls with the broom-stick, and forced them from under the bed to put on their *store clothes*.

When Washington got to the house, dinner was on the table, with unmistakable evidence that a large portion of it had been devoured, and the good lady, not having fully succeeded in removing all the scraps from view, rained on him a pitiless shower of apologies for want of proper preparation to receive him.

"Ef I'd a know'd it was you." said she to the President, "I'd a had some short jonny-cake for you."

The President could only set and smile as the shower of apologies increased in intensity, without attempting to wedge in a word, for she could say fifty to his one. He therefore meekly stood the shower, and Christopher sat on the door-sill with hat in hand, whirling it round and round, smiling at the embarrassing situation of the President.

On the day of his arrival at the old soldier's place of domicil, it was "fish day in the hundred," for the inhabitants at this season of the year, had a *fish-pot* constructed in an adjacent stream, from which each family of the hundred was supplied on alternate days.

A fish pot is constructed by building two stone walls from each bank of any small river, to meet and form an angle in the water at some considerable distance down the stream. At the commencement of cool nights in dog-days, the fish descend the river and seek the deep water at its mouth. As they descend the stream, the two walls compel them to come to the angle at the junction, where the water escapes through a carefully constructed lattice work of wood, in which the large fish are entangled, and can therefore be easily raked into the fisherman's canoe.

The good lady soon invited the President to set down to "corn pone, boiled rock and fried eels," for it was literally fish day in the hundred, and a complete fish dinner was therefore on the table. A few dainties were hastily brought out, and the Chief "sot down to dinner," for he would allow no more apology and no further time to prepare a better dinner.

"I must eat and go," said he, and making himself "quite common," partook heartily of the fish, and the whole family soon became entirely easy in his presence. But there was a manifest want of that gravity and polite demeanor which should characterize a family whose guest was the first President of these United States, yet there existed an excuse for this state of things, which, when explained, might afford an ample apology. Things becoming worse and worse, the good lady was at last forced to an explanation of the irrepressible inclination to laughter, and apparent want of manners in her children, and even in those grown daughters whom she had pummeled with the broom-stick and forced to put on store clothes. She had however to put off the unpleasant task as long as possible, for fear the President "might be mad" if told, but it was no use, for things got worse and worse, and the secret must come out.

"General," said the madam, "I want to tell you something if you don't be mad."

"I hope I will not," replied the General, with a smile, as he continued to eat his fish.

The old lady tremblingly proceeded to tell the President all that happened at the gate, the *capers* of the colt and dogs, and how little Lizzie had affixed a new termination to his name by calling him General Washing*tub*—dreading his anger and coloring in the face all the time.

"I hope," added she, "you won't be mad General, for children will be children at the best o' times."

Washington laughed quite heartily at the singular name little Lizzie had given him, and kindly calling her, he placed her on his knee and fed her with fish from his own plate. The madam soon resumed her shower of apologies for the fish dinner, and the President, resolved on silencing the battery, suddenly laid down his knife and fork, and looking her gravely in the face, said, "If you had all the good things in Kent county, do you think I could eat them all, madam? Your fish dinner is just what suits me, and I would eat nothing else if you should prepare it. Your dinner, madam, is good enough for me."

Those polite, but firm words, effectually silenced the madam, and rising from the table, he placed little Lizzie in his chair to finish her dinner; and patting her on the cheek, said, "Now you can always have it to say that you have dined on the knee of General Washing. *tub.*"

"As he passed along, often would mothers bring their children to look on the paternal Chief, yet not a word was heard of President of the United States; the little innocents were taught to lisp the name of Washington alone. He was rather partial to children; their infantine playfulness appeared to please him, and many are the parents who at this day rejoice that his patriarchal hands have touched their offspring."

Christopher and Fairfax Pompey, had occupied several hours in telling stories; it was now growing late, and Hail Columbia must therefore be sung at once, for the first time, by little Jack's choir. Cully's cottage, about one mile from the mansion of the Chief, was selected by the choir to elude the eye and ear of Miss Nelly, that fun-loving young lady, and musical critic, who would ramble in the groves of Mount Vernon. Little Jack therefore dreaded her presence, for, said he "Dat eye o' hern am too sharp, and she knows jes zactly too much for me."

At this party, wit and anecdote were to have the largest liberty, and Mose, the cow-boy, who boasted of having run the "human race" in chasing a pole-cat, was to have perfect freedom from restraint by the rigid philosophy of the home plantation.

"Move down dar, Dol," said aunt Phillis, who occupied the same bench, "you scrouges me."

"I scrouges you!" exclaimed Dolly, with surprise. "How's I gwine to scrouge you, down dar, I wonders?"

"You scrouges me," replied Phillis, earnestly biting a peach, "dat's all I has to say."

"You spreads and spreads jes like de *wiper* when he's gwine to bite," said Dolly, and up she sprang with a toss of the head, and found a seat on an opposite bench.

"Dat's reely rustycratic," said Phillis. "Se how she puts on de nickletigram swagger."

"O ladies!" said Peter, "you hurts my feelins."

" 'Mortal patriots! rise once more," exclaimed the cow-boy.

"Genblemen and ladies," said Pompey, "dat young man bab swallowed a hard-book."

"His mouf bites at de philosophy o' Bacon," said the collector of the port.

"Dat's a fac," said the schoolmaster, "I seed him eat 'bout free pounds for dinner."

The mirth occasioned by the cow-boy's wit having subsided, and order having been restored, Hail Columbia was struck up, the first stanza was sung with great *eclat*, and a pause ensued.

"Dat's not sung right," said a voice at some distance in the woods, imitating the voice of an African.

"You lies," was the prompt reply of little Jack, understanding the voice to be that of some mischievous African girl.

Quite an earnest, though suppressed, laugh, proceeding from some persons concealed behind trees in the dark, was now audible to little Jack and his musical satellites, and he dismounted from the stand and proceeded in the direction of the party. He had not proceeded far before he was brought to a halt and confronted by a lady, close behind whom stood two attendant gentlemen.

"Miss Nelly, I axes your pardon," said little Jack, humbly removing his singing cap, and the lively laugh of Miss Custis rang through the woods. She had learned from some of the servants at the mansion, that a peach party was being held in the grove of Cully Jr. at which Hail Columbia was to be sung, and she had clandestinely appeared there with Mr. Lear and Mr. Lewis, to hear the music. A plate of fine peaches was soon handed to the uninvited guests, of which they partook and retired. Hail Columbia was soon finished, and the peach party was turned into a dancing party, which continued to a late hour.

This dancing party terminated in the following witticism between Fairfax Pompey and an African belle of Dogue Run.

Pompey said,

> "I vows, nay, I does swear,
> I'll dance wid none but what am fair."

The lady replied—

> "Den 'spose we ladies should dispense,
> Our hands to none but men o' sense."

Pompey stammeringly replied—

> "Den 'spose, well madam, and what den ?"

> "Why, sar, you'd neber dance again,"

replied the belle, and Pompey took his departure from the famous peach party a wiser man.

7

Time swept by, like the restless waters of the ever-changing Potomac, that washes the foot of Mount Vernon, leveling the great Chief in its course, and after the lapse of more than sixty years, the turkey driver of '97 is found a slave for life, selling vegetables to the inhabitants of a small village iu Maryland. Every summer he appears in the village market, the same intelligent and polite old man, as seen in the picture. We were not willing that this old man should totter by us with his story of the past all untold, to the grave, where so many secrets lie buried, for we know that in some chamber of his memory, curtained and cob-webbed, were dust-covered relics of the past, just what the youth of to-day so eagerly seek.

CHAPTER VI.

WE will next notice affairs at Mount Vernon in '99, the last year of the 18th century. It opens with sunshine on the home of Washington; but, as lengthening shadows proclaim its close, other premonitory shadows hurry by; clouds envelop the horizon, and hang the sacred Mount with a pall of gloom. It opens with joy, and the ancient halls "echo to the tread of lovers;" but closes with a cutworm at the root of bliss, withering the fair plants of the Mount, and inclining them to kindred clay. At the beginning a new chain of love is formed, and "bride and bridegroom, pilgrims of life, henceforward to travel together," commenced their journey; but, near the end, a stronger chain, well tried by the force of time, is shattered by the desolator. The great Chief has read up the eventful journal of his life, and is seen no more on the Mount.

At the opening of this year, the following extract of a letter, written to her by Washington in '95, was still fresh in the memory of Miss Nelly Custis:—"Hence it follows that love may and therefore ought to be under the guidance of reason; for, although we cannot avoid first impressions, we may assuredly place them under guard; and my motives for treating on this subject are to show you, while you remain Eleanor Parke Custis, spinster, and retain the resolution to love with moderation, the propriety of adhering to the latter resolution, at least until you have secured your game. When the fire is beginning to kindle, and your heart growing warm, propound these questions to it: Who is this invader? Have I a competent knowledge of him ?   Is he a man of good character ?—a man of sense ?   For, be assured, a sensible woman can never be happy with a fool.   What has been his walk in life ?   Is he a gambler, a spendthrift, or drunkard ?   Is his fortune sufficient to maintain me in the manner I have been accustomed to live, and my sisters do live ?   and is he one to whom my friends can have no reasonable objection ?   If these interrogatories can be satisfactorily answered, there will remain but one more to be asked—that, however, is an important one :   Have I sufficient ground to conclude that his affections are engaged by me ?"

Lawrence Lewis, Washington's favorite nephew, and Miss Eleanor Parke Custis, Mrs. Washington's grand-daughter, were married at Mount Vernon, the 22d February, 1799, Rev. Thomas Davis, of Alexandria, performing the ceremony.   "Three days before, Washington, as her foster-father, wrote from Mount Vernon to the clerk of Fairfax County Court, saying :   'Sir, you will please to grant a license for the marriage of Eleanor Parke Custis with Lawrence Lewis ; and this shall be your authority for so doing.'"

.The marriage took place on Friday, "a bright and beautiful day. The early spring flowers were budding in the hedges, and the blue-bird, making its way cautiously northward, gave a few joyous notes in the garden that morning.   The occasion was one of great hilarity at Mount Vernon, for the bride was beloved by all, and Major Lewis, the bridegroom, had ever been near the heart of his uncle, since the death of his mother, who so much resembled her illustrious brother, that it was a matter of frolic to throw a cloak around her, and placing a military hat on her head, such was the amazing resemblance, that, on her appearance, battalions would have presented arms, and senates risen to do homage to the Chief."

At the time of her marriage, Miss Nelly was one month less than twenty years of age.   "She was considered one of the most beautiful women of the day, to which her portrait at Arlington House, by Gilbert Stewart, bears testimony."

When Aunt Betty was informed that a wedding was about to come off at Mount Vernon, at which her cooking abilities would be severely taxed, she said to Aunt Phillis, her rival, "I bounds I'se gwine to hab dat greasy meal all right."

"Yes," replied Aunt Phillis, "I specs you will, if you's well watched. Hark, he gwine to be sont for, I hears."

"Ef Hark come foolin,' 'long wid me," replied Aunt Betty, "he gwine to see sumpin. I soon send all sich dandy niggers to hoein' 'taters in de land o' Nod," and off she flew to her dishes, which she handled in the most polished style.

Washington's chief cook at Philadelphia, during the two terms of the presidency, "was named Hercules, and familiarly termed Uncle Harkless. Trained in the mysteries of his art from early youth, and in the palmy days of Virginia, when her thousand chimneys smoked to indicate the generous hospitality that reigned throughout the whole length and breadth of her wide domain, Uncle Harkless was at the period of the first presidency, as highly accomplished a proficient in the culinary art as could be found in the United States. He was a dark-brown man, little, if any, above the usual size, yet possessed of such great muscular power as to enable him to be compared with his namesake of fabulous history.

"The chief cook gloried in the cleanliness and nicety of his kitchen. Under his iron discipline, wo to his underlings if speck or spot could be discerned on the tables or dressers, or if the utensils did not shine like polished silver. With the luckless wights who had offended in these particulars, there was no arrest of punishment, for judgment and execution went hand in hand. The steward, and indeed the whole household, treated the chief cook with much respect, as well for his valuable services as for his general good character and pleasing manners.

"It was while preparing the Thursday, or Congress dinner, that Uncle Harkless shone in all his splendor. During his labors upon this banquet, he required some half dozen aprons, and napkins out of number. It was surprising the order and discipline that was observed in so bustling a scene. His underlings flew in all directions to execute his orders, while he, the great master-spirit, seemed to possess the power of ubiquity and to be everywhere at the same moment. When the steward in snow-white apron, silk shorts and stockings, and hair in full powder, placed the first dish on the table, the clock being on the stroke of four, the 'labors of Hercules' ceased.

"While the masters of the republic were engaged in discussing the savory viands of the Congress dinner, the chief cook retired to make

7*

his toilet for an evening promenade. His perquisites from the slops of the kitchen were from one to two hundred dollars a year. Though homely in person, he lavished most of these large avails upon dress. In making his toilet, his linen was of unexceptionable whiteness and quality, then black silk shorts, ditto waistcoat, ditto stockings, shoes highly polished, with large buckles covering a considerable part of the foot, blue cloth coat with velvet collar and bright metal buttons, a long watch chain dangling from his fob, a cocked hat, and gold-headed cane, completed the grand costume of the celebrated dandy of the President's kitchen.

"Thus arrayed, the chief cook invariably passed out at the front door, the porter making a low bow, which was promptly returned. Joining his brother loungers of the pave, he proceeded up market street, attracting considerable attention, that street being, in the old times, the resort where fashionables 'did most congregate.' Many were not a little surprised on beholding so extraordinary a personage, while others who knew him would make a formal and respectful bow, that they might receive in turn the salute of one of the most polished gentlemen and the veriest dandy of sixty years ago."

On the wedding night, Thomas, the ex-turkey-driver of '97, now a skillful assistant in Frank's department, had the pleasure of seeing the "banquet table sot," and "neber seed the likes afore. It was 'yand all wonders in dis world 'cep one," and that was when "Mose and Tom, and another nigger, and two more hounds, kotch another raccoon and two more pole-cats."

"Marse, he sot in one corner," said an old servant that enjoyed a peep, "and Missus, she sot siden him; Miss Nelly, she sot in tudder corner, and Marse Lewis, he sot siden her, and de party eat and drunk, and played, and danced all ober de house till most day-light.'

. "It was my intention before this," writes one of the guests, "to have given some little account of the wedding, (which was accomplished without the ceremony of the ring,) of the supper, &c., which, from the commodiousness of the parlor, gave it a most pleasing appearance. The table was in the form of a T, at which near forty persons sat down, and was well spread with the choicest viands, wines, pastry, &c—plenty without profusion, and neatly arranged. The minister partook, and stayed to cut up a large pound-cake, of about twelve pounds, part of which he ran through a ring and afforded some amusement to the groomsmen and bridesmaids, who wrapped it up in paper, and handed it round to the company, reserving enough of the magic-cake for their succeeding slumbers—but what were their dreams, I already presume you neither expect to hear, nor that it would be in my power to tell—nay, I fancy you must smile at the idea when I am at this moment' so much puzzled to give any tolerable detail of what occupied both my hands, and that without intermission, for a week. While the groomsmen were employed in making punch, and introducing the gentlemen to the banquet, consisting of two large rounds of beef, several tongues, and hams with plenty of olives, bread, wine and cheese, our bridesmaids in the adjoining room, sung and played beautifully. Tea, lemonade and wine, music and a country dance, closed the scene, and the company to the number of about fifty, began to go."

On the next evening after the wedding, there assembled on the lawn, within hearing of the bride and bridegroom, the famous choir of Little Jack, to give a serenade. Though the night air was keen and frosty, yet the rich notes of the native African voice rang harmoniously, soaring over the lofty trees around the happy mansion of Mount Vernon. Washington had now reached the 67th anniversary of his birth, his accomplished adopted daughter was now settled in life, and to celebrate these events in the history of the Mount, the old colonial bridal song, dating long before the revolution, was beautifully sung and repeated by the choir. A verse or two:

"Down de vale o' life I tends,
  Whar hoary age creeps slowly on;
And wid de burdening thought I bends,
  Dat youf and all its joys am gone.

"Let mopin' monks and ramblin' rakes,
  De joys ob wedded life deride;
Dar 'pinions rise from gross mistakes,
  Unbridled brains and gloomy pride.

"Thy sacred sweets, O 'nubial love,
  Flow from de 'fections more refined;
De 'fections sacred to de dove,
  Heroic, constant, warm and kind.

"Hail! holy flame! hail! sacred tie,
What binds two gentle souls in one;
On equal wings dar sorrows fly,
In equal streams dar pleasures run.

"Dar duties still dar pleasures bring,
Hence joys in quick succession come;
A queen am she, he am a king,
And dar dominion am dar home."

Here a white handkerchief was waved from an upper window of the mansion, approving the serenade and the choir full of joy at its appearance, retired to their homes for the night.

The spring of '99 opened with unusual beauty and life at Mount Vernon, and every creature, full of melody, appeared to enjoy a perfect pleasure. A life unknown to other estates was lived and enjoyed under the mild and firm rule of the Chief of the Mount, and a cheerful spirit performed more than half the labor in the fields, and at the mansion. It was during this spring that a song called the "Wren Song, or Washington rules in the great Western World," was written, and sung by the choirs at Mount Vernon; and, like Hail Columbia of the previous year, it promised to eclipse all other songs for the season. The breezes of the Mount had borne along many a thrilling melody and comic strain, but the "Wren Song," combining all the wild notes of the native African, beautifully blended, gave out tones of the grave anthem, the comic carol, and the sprightly notes of the wren, singularly reduced to the most perfect harmony. The tune of the Wren Song has been lost in the din of time, but the words almost as true as the original, are still repeated, though more than half a century has left its traces on the brain that has preserved them. A few lines are remembered—

Chitter litter, chitter litter, lee-lee-lee,
Old Britain is conquered, Columbia is free;
Our foes have been vanquished, the tyrant is hurled,
And Washington rules in the great western world;
Sounds of our freedom the breezes are bringing,
The wren in the orchard of Liberty is singing.
He lights on the limb of a hollow peach tree,
And there sings a sonnet, Columbia is free.

Chorus.—Cheer up Jinny ! come into tea,
   The peach tree's blooming, chitter litter, lee ;
   Chitter litter, chitter litter, lee-lee-lee,
   Peach orchard, ree-ree-ree.

Chitter litter, chitter litter, lee-lee-lee,
Our children are living our freedom to see,
Our standard is planted, our banner unfurled,
And Washington rules in the great western world ;
Nobly the emblem of freedom is flying,
The thunder of war in the distance is dying ;
But France, that proud nation, may yet live to see
The strength of our navy—Columbia is free.

Chitter litter, chitter litter, lee-lee-lee,
Our heroes immortal, the brave and the free ;
The wheels of our great revolution have whirled,
And Washington rules in the great western world ;
From ocean to ocean our standard is planting,
And "long live the Chief," a free people are chanting ;
The ships of our commerce shall cover the sea,
Like swift-shooting stars, for Columbia is free.

Chitter litter, chitter litter, lee-lee-lee,
Come rest in the shade of our Liberty tree ;
By treason's sirocco no leaf shall be curled,
For Washington rules in the great western world.
Our freedom has set the crowned head to reflecting,
And men the divine right of kings are rejecting,
And claiming our land an asylum to be,
For all the oppressed, for Columbia is free.

Chitter litter, chitter litter, lee-lee-lee,
A warning to traitors forever shall be,
Our bright starry banner will never be furled,
For Washington rules in the great western world ;
The steel of Columbia will ever be gleaming,
As long as an Arnold of treason is dreaming ;
Then take root and flourish, O Liberty tree !
For Washington still lives—Columbia is free.

Chorus.—Cheer up Jinny ! come in to tea,
The peach tree's blooming, chitter litter, lee;
Chitter litter, chitter litter, lee-lee-lee,
Peach orchard, ree-ree-ree."

Almost without a single exception, in every song sung at Mount Vernon in the olden time, some appropriate allusion was made to the American flag; its history and symbolic significations were recorded in every brain; and it was considered a shame for any servant to grow up to the age of seven years without a knowledge of the history of the great Chief and his flag.

O that we *could* write its history; that we could record it in every brain; that we could stereotype it on every heart; that we could engrave it on the eternal flint of words to live forever; for we know that while those monuments which pierce the skies in honor of the great Chief shall endure, his flag will never lose a star; and though one or more may suffer obscuration for a season, yet the cloudy veil will soon be torn asunder, and every star shall shine again in all its pride and glory, till the eventful journal of time shall be read up to its conclusion.

"In March, 1775," says the American Encyclopædia, "a union flag with a red field, was hoisted upon the liberty pole in New York, with the inscription, 'George Rex, and the Liberties of America.' The Connecticut troops bore upon their standards and drums, the arms of the colony, with the motto, *Qui transtulit sustinet;* and by act of the provincial congress, the standard of each regiment was distinguished by its color, as for the seventh, blue; for the eighth, orange, &c. The flag displayed by General Putnam, on Prospect Hill, near Boston, July 18, 1775, was red, in token of defiance, and bore on one side the motto of Connecticut, and on the other the words: 'An appeal to Heaven,' which were adopted by a resolution of the provincial congress of Massachusetts, April 29, 1776, as the motto to be borne on the flag of the cruisers of that colony—a white flag with a green pine tree. The first American flag unfurled in South Carolina, a blue ground with a white crescent in the dexter corner, was designed by Col. Moultrie, at the request of the council of safety, and was carried at the taking of Fort Johnston, September 13, 1775. By a letter of Col. Joseph Reed, October 20, 1775, it appears that the flag of the floating batteries was similar to that of the Massachusetts cruisers. The standard of the first American fleet was hoisted at Philadelphia, December 22, 1775, by Paul Jones, with his own hands, as Commodore Ezekiel Hopkins embarked on board his flag ship, the Alfred; it represented a rattle snake on a yellow field, with the motto: 'Don't tread on me'—a device suggested probably by the head pieces of many of the newspapers in the revolutionary interest, in which a disjointed snake divided into thirteen parts, with the motto: 'Join or die,' was employed to typify the necessity of union. When this result had been accomplished, the device was changed into a united snake, or into a rattle-snake about to strike. The fleet did not sail from the Delaware capes until February 17, 1776, when it carried the flag known as the 'Great Union,' which was first displayed by Washington upon the heights before Boston, upon assuming the command of the newly organized army of the colonies, January 1, 1776, and which consisted of the crosses of St. George and St. Andrew, on a blue ground in the upper corner, with a field composed of alternate horizontal stripes of red and white, to indicate the union of the colonies for the maintenance of their rights within the empire of Great Britain. The combination of these two colors was probably suggested by the red flag of the army and the white one of the navy, previously in use, and the form of stripes by the order of Washington that officers of different grades should wear stripes of different colors to prevent mistakes, and to enable 'both officers and men to make themselves acquainted with the persons of all officers in general command.' The emblems of British union having become inappropriate after the declaration of independence, it was ordered by Congress, June 14, 1777, 'that the flag of the thirteen United States be thirteen stripes, alternate red and white; that the Union be thirteen stars, white in a blue field, representing a new constellation.' It is not known precisely to whom is due the credit of suggesting the stars for the Union. The idea is supposed to have emanated from John Adams, who was then chairman of the board of war; and it has also been urged with considerable plausibility, that the stars and stripes of the national standard were borrowed from the coat of arms of the Washington family, the shield of which presents a white or silver field traversed by two red bars, with three spur rowels or stars in the upper portion. The resolution of June 14, was not made public until September 3, 1777, and the stars and stripes first figured conspicuously at the surrender of Burgoyne in the succeeding month; in December of the same year they were carried to Europe by Paul Jones in his ship, the Ranger."

The thirteen stars and stripes remained on the flag until April 4, 1818, when Congress passed an act providing that a new star shall be added on the fourth of July next succeeding the admission of any new state into the Union—and so may the stars continue to increase until "this whole boundless continent is ours."

"Washington's Life Guard was formed in 1776, soon after the siege of Boston, while the American army was encamped in York, or Manhattan Island, near the city of New York. Caleb Gibbs, of Rhode Island, was its first chief, and bore the title of *Captain Lieutenant.* He held that office until the close of 1779, when he was succeeded by William Colfax, one of his Lieutenants. Gibbs's lieutenants were Henry P. Livingston, of New York, William Colfax, of New Jersey, and Benjamin Grymes, of Virginia.

"During the maritime war with France," says Mr. Custis, of Arlington, "the armed merchantmen that sailed from Alexandria would salute on passing Mount Vernon. On the report of the gun, the General would leave his library, and taking a position in the portico that fronts the river, remain there uncovered, till the firing ceased. And yet another salute awakened the echoes around the shores of Mount Vernon; another act of homage was paid to the retired Chief; and this was the homage of the heart, for it was paid by an old companion-in-arms, while its echoes called up the memories of the past. A small vessel would be seen to skim along the bosom of the Potomac. Nearing the shore the little craft furled her sails, let go her anchor, and discharged a small piece of ordnance; then a boat put off and pulled to the shore, and soon a messenger appeared, bearing a fine rock or drum fish, with the compliments of Benjamin Grymes, who resided some fifty miles down the river, and who was a gallant officer of the Life-Guard in the war of the Revolution."

Mr. Custis became the owner of the flag of the Life-Guard. "The flag is of white silk, on which the device is neatly painted. One of the guard is seen holding a horse, and in the act of receiving a flag from the Genius of Liberty, who is personified as a woman leaning on the union shield, near which is the American eagle. The motto of the corps, 'conquer or die,' is upon a ribbon. The uniform of the guard consisted of a blue coat with white facings, white waistcoat and breeches, black half gaiters, and a cocked hat with blue and white feathers. They carried muskets and occasionally small arms."

At the assault on Spring Hill redoubt, siege of Savannah, 9th October, 1779, "terrible was the conflict at this point just as the day dawned. The French column led to the assault, were confronted by a blaze of musketry from the redoubt, and by a cross-fire from the adjoining batteries. Whole ranks were mowed down like grass before the scythe. The American standards were those of the second South Carolina regiment, embroidered and sent to them by Mrs. Susanna Elliott, three days after the battle of Fort Moultrie in 1776, and were planted by Lieutenants Hume and Bush. The French standard was raised by one of D'Estaing's aides, who, with Hume and Bush, soon fell mortally wounded, leaving their colors fluttering in the breeze. Lieutenant Gray, of the South Carolina regiment, seeing his associates fall, seized the standards and kept them erect, when he too was prostrated by a bullet. Serjeant Jasper sprang forward, secured the colors, and had just fastened them upon the parapet, when a rifle ball pierced him, and he fell into the ditch. Just before he died he said to Major Horry, 'Tell Mrs. Elliott I lost my life supporting the colors she presented to our regiment.' "

On the third day after the battle of Fort Moultrie on Sullivan's Island, in 1776, Mrs. Elliott presented the flag above referred to, to the second South Carolina regiment, commanded by Col. Moultrie. On the authority of the United States Gazette for February, 1779, it is stated that Col. Moultrie in his speech receiving the flag, said to his men, "my gallant companions! you see the advantage of courage and fortitude—you have fought and have conquered, and the brave fellows who fell in the cannonade of yesterday, *are now in heaven riding in their chariots like the devil."*

Ever on the alert, and behind in nothing, the city of Boston, side by side with New York, and her noble Yankee boys fast falling into line, began to arm for the contest, and sing her war songs during the French troubles of '98.

The following was the patriotic song of Boston, to the tune of "To Anacreon in Heaven," an old English Bacchanalian song, dating back to about the year 1795.

"Ye sons of Columbia, who bravely have fought
    For those rights, which unstained from your sires had descended,
May you long taste the blessings your valor has bought,
    And your sons reap the soil which your fathers defended;
'Mid the reign of mild peace, may your nation increase
With the glory of Rome, and the wisdom of Greece;
    And ne'er may the sons of Columbia be slaves,
    While the earth bears a plant or the sea rolls in waves.

"Should the tempest of war overshadow our land,
    Its bolts could ne'er rend freedom's temple asunder,
For, unmoved at its portal, would Washington stand,
    And repulse with his breast the assaults of the thunder!
His sword from the sleep of its scabbard would leap,
And conduct with its point, every flash to the deep."

Two stanzas will suffice. This song, written by a Boston poet in '98, has the honor of the first patriotic American "Anacreon" on record in the United States. England had many songs which she sung to the same air, but they were all of a bacchanalian character; and America enjoyed the honor of first wresting the beautiful air "To Anacreon in Heaven," from English bacchanalians, while Washington yet lived, and threw it to the wings of the breeze to convey the noble sentiments of American Liberty to every American heart.

And Pennsylvania, never behind—not even New York and Boston—in her country's trials in '98, began to sing in Philadelphia, the second patriotic Anacreon on record in the United States. A verse or two:

"Ye sons of Columbia, determined to keep
    Those choice blessings and rights, that for years have descended
From the battles and blood of your sires—who now sleep,
    And who gained by the sword, what with life they defended:
Swear and shout in the song, in a strain loud and long,
Until heaven, like earth, shall its echoes prolong—
    That ne'er shall Columbia be robbed of a right,
    While the sun rules the day, or the moon rules the night.

"And has not great Washington offered again,
  To lead and to march in support of our nation ;
Then Americans, rouse l to the field and the main,
  And crush every wretch that opposes your station.
Let your cannon and sword, all protection afford,
Show your firmness, your courage, so famed, so adored,
  Swear, ne'er shall Columbia be robbed of a right,
  While the sun rules the day or the moon rules the night."

On the 4th of July, 1799, the choir of Mount Vernon celebrated
in song the anniversary of American Independence, and after singing Hail Columbia, the New York, Boston and Philadelphia patriotic songs, the latter two to the air "To Anacreon in Heaven," the
American flag of '77, the flag of Washington and the fathers of the
Republic, floating in all its pride and glory over the heads of the
choir, was thus addressed by Scomberry, the sage of Dogue Run—

"King George, de king o' Britain, and all de army o' red-coats
what Washington and de fathers ob dis nation flogged from de
Quebec to de Floridas, 'magined in his dreams o' bliss dat yon flag
never gwine to float ober dis mountain. He 🖔magined also dat he
gwine to raise de mos 'normous flock o' tarkeys on dis continent,
'ticlarly round about de town o' Bostin whar de pilgrims fust sot foot
on de shores ob de new world, and what promised to 'come a mos
'digious roostin' place, where he fully 'spected to find de mos 'stoun-
din' nest ob eggs ebery season, 'sides good shootin' in de fall ob de
year. Dis hab bin de practice o' tyrants eber sense de sabages
burnt de hard-books at Alexandria in de kingdom ob de 'Gyptians,
and Nero sot fire to de city o' Rome. He 'magined he gwine to
send de huntsmen wid hounds and ole muskets to de colony o' Bostin right in de season, rob de nests and kill de ole tarkeys jes when
he mine to, and make 'em smoke on de table o' parlyment o' Britain.
But jes 'fore many seasons rolled round, or 'fore many moons riz
and sot in de horizontal o' Boston, de ole tarkeys 'gan to 'come tired
o' loosin' all dar eggs and ob de tax on dar corn widout de 'quiva-
lent for stainin' life and feedin' de young ones ; so de ole gobblers
'bout de town o' Bostin, seein' all dar corn and some 'normous bas-
kets ob eggs and bags o' feathers gwine ober de 'Lantic, 'gan to stick
up dar feathers jes like de quills ob de huge porkinpine, and go
gobble ! gobble ! gobble ! jes like dey gwine to fight; but de king

acted jes like he gwine to pay no attention to dis under no probom-
focation whatsomebber, and at las' sont a big ship 'cross de 'Lantic
loaded wid boxes o' tea wid de most 'normous long tax bills wid de
boxes you eber seed sense 'Curgus spounded law in de Greece. De
ole gobblers soon 'gan to stride round de town o' Bostin wid de
longest kind o' strides, and said we not gwine to eat dat tea no how
you gwine to fix it; we wants corn, and we wants to send an ole
gobbler ober de 'Lantic to gobble for us in de parlyment o' Britain.
De king said no, I'se 'posed to dat, genblemen, you's my humble-
sarvant gobblers; I wants no continental gobblers in dis rustycratic
parlyment o' mine. I'se gwine to tax you widout representation.
De ole tarkeys now ran right off to de tree o' Liberty, and sot up
dat flag, some runnin' and some flyin,' and some bofe, and jes sot
right down in de shade and 'gan to gobble like a grabe council o'
'liberators, and you neber seed de likes 'fore nor sense de 'treat ob
de glorious ten thousand from the probince o' Babylon. Nex de ole
tarkeys bounced right up, painted their snouts jes like Injuns, jumped
right into de king's ship, and upsot de boxes o' tea right into de harbor o' Bostin! and you nebber seed de likes sense de Romans fit
Gen. Hannibal in Africa. De king soon got riled at dis kind o' 'ceed-
ins', and sont a big army ob red-coats to shoot all de ole gobblers in
de city o' Bostin Soon as de tarkeys 'gan to hear ob dis army ob
red-coats wid ole muskets and rusty ram-rods 'trudin' outen de muz-
zle, de mos 'normous gang o' 'furiated gobblers you eber seed, 'gan to
'semble round de town, spread dar tails, stick up dar heads, and
dare de king's red-coats to pull de trigger One night, howsomeber,
when de ole king and all de parlyment lay sound a snorin' in dar
feather beds picked from de tarkey roosts in America, de army o' red
coats marched right outen Bostin, sot fire to Charlestown, sprised de
tarkey roost at Lexington and Concord, sayin', ''Sperse ye rebels!
come down from dat roost and 'sperse, I says, and, pullin de trigger,
killed and crippled more'n a dozen young gobblers. You nebber
seed de likes o' dis sense Cæsar gobbled up Pompey at de battle o'
Pharsalia. De thunders ob rebolution now shook de parlyment o'
Britain, and de ole king George jumped up jes like a stuck pig, and
found his *tarkeys all done gone !*

"De sarcumstances I has to deal wid to-day 'pells me to pass ober
de days when Nimrod, de mighty grand-daddy o' fox hunters,

cleaned dis ball ob all varmints 'noxious to dis human race; when Job writ wid de iron pen in de 'tarnal 'glyphics; when de Greeks rode rite into de city o' Troy on wooden horses widout saddles and bridles, and ran out de prince wid de gods upon his back; when Solon writ laws in de Greece wid a 'normous long goose quill; when king Ptolemy Pharaoh sot on de 'Gyptian throne, and when Gen. Antony sot out to spark de queen; when Cyrus flogged de king o' Babylon at de supper table for drinking wine to de wicked gods; when Job 'tended a farm in de land ob Uz; and de king o' Bucknazzar eat grass like de oxen; when 'Sandy, de great, licked de Parsians on de banks o' Granicus; when de philosopher whose name I can't say, sot siden de road in a washin-tub; when de ghos met Brutus at Phillippi; when Zeno sot up school on de porch; and when de king o' Parsia chucked a log-chain in de sea o' Hellespont.

"I passes ober all de written treasures ob de ole antiquity dat outlibed the wreck ob mighty empires; ob de palaces ob princes and de temples ob de gods. I closes and passes ober de hard-books whar wisdom speaks in thunder; ober de sublime genius ob de poet what waters the thirsty mind from age to age; and de matchless orations what roused de nations to arms, and chained de senates to de chariot-wheels of speech and sot 'em gwine, and drug de kings ob de earth behind. On de wheels ob mind I drives ober de billows ob old oshun, and shakes de wolcano at my feet; and now I sets de foot o' mighty genius on de rock o' pilgrims, the plains o' Lexington, Concord, Monmouth, and de Yorktown, and stops at Mount Vernon, de classic eye o' Columbia, and feels prouder under dat flag dan he what drug Neighbor-Bucknazzar from his throne!

"Dat flag am de mornin' star o' glorious banners. It was fust histed in de day-break ob 'Merican freedom, and is hailed in ebery land, on ebery sea, and in ebery clime under de spangled canopy ob de heaven, dat sports in de dazzlin' sun-light o' cibilization. O flag, let us neber surrender thee while the silent waters ob dat mighty riber rolls down to de tarnal ocean at its mouf. Dat flag am consecrated in ebery American bosom what glows wid de signs o' life and toats de embers of hope. It am de type and de emblem ob all what am noble, troofful and mighty. It am glorious, heroic, free, and sublime in de history ob dis 'lightened generation. Millions ob hearts hab quibbered wid delight 'neaf its beauteous folds. Dyin'

8°

eyes hab growed bright as de las gaze 'pinged agin its colors. By de light flamin' froo de 'mosphere ob death, in de dark hours ob dis country's history, it has nerved de arm what was 'bout to falter, and 'spired hope in de mountains ob despair. From its stars, brightness has flashed twart de horizontal ob dis mighty ball, kindled de council-fires ob freedom, and sot de chunks a blazin'. It am de flag o' Washington and de conscript fathers ob liberty. Great flag! how I loves you. Come to de 'braces ob my arms. You seed de sufferins' at Walley Forge. Mos awful tyrant-tamer! you scourges traitors! O flag! I lifts my hand and 'treats you in de name o' freedom to sing, shine, and lib foreber. When I thinks ob you, de thoughts ob former years crawl ober my soul like de speckled snake ober de sleeper. Mighty flag! you skeers the world, and puts de fierce Philistine to flight. Kings take to dar heels at de dawn ob yonr star-light; de swift footed ghos ob treason cuts and runs, and de departed red-coat wanderin' here and dar, split for de grabe yard. O flag! you's a baby yet, but you's able to flog Samson. O stars and stripes! you was only born in '77; you's not ob age, hardiy, but 'fore de morn o' 'dependence riz, dat sarcumpolar orb what 'cumgyrates round de axletree ob de world, you gib de signal for de night march, and 'pealed to heben for jestice and got de answer. Marblous flag! de impostles ob liberty cut up dar shirts to make you, and den rocked de cradle o' liberty siden you. O flag! you shall wave from de ribbers to de eend ob de world. I axes you what dis mean? You hesitates—you doubts—I 'spounds de meanin'. It shall be fus planted on de rocky shore ob dis mighty roarin' 'Tomac ribber, den two 'normous eagles wid eyes like fire, and E. Pluribus *Union* in dar claws, shall fly bofe ways, one to de arctic and tudder to de 'tartic pole, den wid one ob de mos 'normous screams, fly up, and up, and up, and histe dat noble banner on bofe de norf and souf poles, den out will peep dat genbleman in de moon, 'mazed at de awful sight—and I tells you dat kings and prophets, lawyers and hypocrites will desire to see de sight what he secs but neber can!"

With Scomberry's great speech we bid adieu to the year '99, and to Mount Vernon for the present. Palestine had her sacred mountains whose history thrills the nations of the world ; she has her sacred caves, where the dust of her warriors, patriarchs, and holy prophets, has reposed for ages ; and to this day the cave of Machpelah, and the sepulchre of Arimathea, are pointed out to the dust-covered pilgrim of all nations : and in this year of '99, the last year of the century, Mount Vernon becomes a sacred Mount, and, like Machpelah, the repository of the dust of the "Father of the Faithful," it becomes the depository of the dust of the "Father of his Country." From this year, as ages roll on, and unborn generations occupy and perish from the world, Mount Vernon will become dearer and dearer to every American heart. The year of '99, bequeaths the name of Washington as a national property where all sympathies throughout one widely extended and diversified republic, will forever meet in unison. From this year, in all dissensions and amid all the storms of party, his precepts will more powerfully speak from the grave with a paternal appeal : and his name, revered by all, will form a stronger and more universal tie of brotherhood.

CHAPTER VII.

Bacchus, the god of wine—Anacreon, the Poet—Anacreontic Verse— English Bacchanalian Lyrics—American Drinking Songs— African Bacchanalians—"To Anacreon in Heaven"—Ralph Tomlinson—"Star Spongled Banner"—Invasion and Capture of Washingon in 1814—Destruction of Public Buildings—Battle of Bladensburg—Invasion of Baltimore—Fort McHenry— "Rockets' red glare"—Francis S. Key—"The Star Spangled Banner" imperishable.

BACCHUS, styled the god of wine, was the son of Jupiter and Semele, daughter of Cadmus. On a voyage to the Island of Naxos, Bacchus fell into the hands of Tyrrhenian pirates, who bound him with cords, intending to sell him as a slave. But the cords fell from his limbs, vines with clustering grapes spread over the sail, and ivy, laden with berries, ran up the masts and sides of the vessel. The god, thereupon assuming the form of a lion, seized the captain of the ship, and the terrified crew, to escape him, leaped into the sea and became dolphins. The pilot alone, who had taken the part of Bacchus, remained on board; the god then declared to him who he was, and took him under his protection. He discovered the culture of the grape vine, and the mode of extracting the precious liquor from the fruit. Bacchus became a great warrior, and India, in particular, was the scene of his conquests. He marched at the head of an army composed of both men and women, and inspired all with divine fury, and armed with clashing cymbals and other musical instruments, and uttering the wildest cries. His conquests were easy and without bloodshed; the nations readily submitted, and the god taught them the use of the vine, the cultivation of the earth, and the art of making honey.

Anacreon, the great master of Bacchanalian song, was born at Teos, a city of Ionia, in the early part of the sixth century before the Christian era. He attained the age of eighty-five years, and the popular opinion is that he died from suffocation in consequence of swallowing a grape-stone while in the act of drinking wine.

"The first Bacchanalian songs were the hymns sung at the Greek mysteries and festivals of Bacchus. Those of the earliest age, still bearing the impress of an oriental origin, specimens of which occur in the orphic and similar hymns, are dignified and mystical. When, however, these solemn rites became more public, and gradually changed to maddening orgies, the character of the song changed also. Then, as Faber informs us, the worshipers strove to urge each other to excesses of daring licentiousness."

"The drinking songs of Anacreon have all the gayety of their subject, without any of its grossness. His assumed philosophy, however irrational in itself, gives a dignity to his manner; and there is a pathos in the thought, of fleeting life, which perhaps constitutes the secret charm of many of these effusions of voluptuousness. Greek poetry relating to wine and Bacchus appears to have expired with the collossal effort of Nonus of Egypt, who, in the fifth century wrote forty-eight books of Dionysiacs, in which, singularly enough, we have a return to the old faith which makes Bacchus the great central god. Of all the Romans, Horace was, however, emphatically the Bacchanalian poet, commending drinking in a downright manner previously unknown to the luxurious orientalized wine-singers of antiquity. The middle ages were, however, prolific in wild drinking songs, the most celebrated being that by Walter Mapes, written in the twelfth century, and sung to this day in German universities." A few verses from the American Encyclopædia:

"Brightest souls on earth below have by the goblet thriven,
Hearts imbued by nectar strong to realms above are driven;
Sweeter tastes my wine to me in a tavern'given,
Than the Bishop's pious tap well with water shriven.

"All my verses have the smack of the liquor by me,
But if you would see me write, with a supper try me!
Till I've had a bite or two I am never rhymey,
But with half a dozen cups Ovid can't come nigh me.

"Nature hath to every man proper gifts allotted,
Fasting I can never write, nor unless besotted;
Hungry, even by a boy I might be garrotted
Ere I'd thirst I'd let me first in a hearse be trotted.

"In my soul the sparkling fount of prophecy outwelling,
Ne'er was felt until with wine my every vein was swelling,
But when Bacchus in my brain holds his lordly dwelling,
Phœbus rushes into me glorious marvels telling."

"For the credit of Mapes it should be stated that he puts this song into the confession of a beau ideal of a reprobate."

"It would be impossible to give with any accuracy, an idea of the Bacchanalian minstrelsy of France, so prolific and yet so fleeting is its character; modern Italy has never been a land eminent in drinking songs, and its Bacchanalian lyrics generally are modeled after the classics, or in more recent days, after the French; but it may be fairly claimed that, of all languages, the English possesses at least the greatest variety of these lyrics. In its earlier stages it abounds with jovial, hearty staves, dedicated it is true, rather to Cambrinus, the saint of ale, than to Bacchus. Need we speak of Shakespeare and the revelers of the Mermaid, all of whom gave forth their drinking songs or catches so merrily? or of Herrick, who lacked but little of being the English Anacreon. The Jacobite songs of a later era, though political, are all desperately steeped in wine and strong waters, but it is first in Burns that we find a revival of the hearty old English drinking lyric. In America, where men sing less 'at table than elsewhere, some popular Bacchanalian songs have been produced, but they can hardly be said to form a distinct or original department in the literature of the country."

The early part of the present century can, however, boast of one spirited Bacchanalian song which "lived beloved and died regretted" by all who knew it, and loved a gin-soaked brain better than I. It departed this life during the presidency of Jackson, and now appears to be silently sleeping beyond "that bourne whence no traveler returns." A verse—

"Let the farmer praise his grounds, and the huntsman praise his
        hounds,
    And the parson praise the world that's to come,
But whatever comes to pass, my religion's in a glass,
    So baptise me in a hogshead of rum, rum, rum, rum,
    So baptise me in a hogshead of rum."

The American negro is never behind, but if at all permitted, he keeps in sight of his master, doing whatever is done, and singing whatever is sung. He gaily sings his sentimental, comic, and Bacchanalian song, and in those, apes the white man, as well as in all the other refined courtesies of life. We have an instance of a sable disciple of Bacchus, and a cotemporary of ex-President Jefferson, at Monticello, returning from a village ho-down in Virginia, with jug closely in his embraces, when suddenly he was taken with a *miscellaneous mixture of the legs*, and brought to a halt among thick grape vines at a late hour of the night. Uptripped by the rebellious vines, yet hugging his jug as his only hope, and indulging in pleasing reflections concerning his smiling little decanter at home, he is made to break the solitudes of night, and sing—

> I axes what am dat, am dat what ails me,
>   I'se tangled in de wines ;
> My knees am 'bout, yes, jes 'bout gwine to fail me,
>   Ob grog I has de signs.
>
> Chorus.—Hi, ho, my bottle,
>   So cheerin' and so gay ;
>   We started home together,
>   But now we's lost de way.
>
> I axes what am dat, am dat what ails me,
>   I staggers as I walks ;
> My head am turnin', turnin' all around me,
>   I stutters as I talks.
>
> I axes does I hug, I hug dis bottle,
>   O yes I'se sure I does ;
> But what am dat, am dat what ails me,
>   My ears begin to buz.
>
> I axes you for one more pull sweet bottle ;
>   O speak, I fears you's def :
> I has dis 'normous, 'normous buzzin',
>   I'se got so short o' breff.
>
> I feels a shakin' chill, a chill all ober,
>   I can't sleep here o' nights ;
> I'se haunted, haunted by de ghoses ;
>   And sees mos shockin' sights.

I axes why sich things, sich things, I wonders,
   Do 'flict dis human race ;
What make dat, make dat beauty sparkle,
   In dat decauter's face.

Ise gwine, I says, I says, to read de planets,
   Dis night if freezin' keen ;
Ise gwine to 'sult, to 'sult de *hard-books*,
   To know what all dis mean.

I says I has been tricked, and tricked and conjured,
   And 'countered scrapes before ;
Ise been uptripped and knocked, knocked under,
   But not like dis Ise sure.

Chorus.—Hi, ho, my bottle,
   So cheerin' and so gay ;
   We started home together,
   But now we's lost de way.

Leaving the sable Bacchanalian of Monticello to extricate himself from the vines of Bacchus as best he can, and find his way home, we go back to England, and call up one of her drinking lyrics—a song destined to trouble the Siloam of patriotism for many ages to come. Ralph Tomlinson, an English poet of whom very little is known, has left on record a song whose *air* and *measure* of verse have formed the ground-work of a mighty monument of American patriotism. The music cannot be traced to its author, but it has been nationalized on this side of the Atlantic to live while American freedom endures. We mean the English Bacchanalian song, "To Anacreon in Heaven."

William H. Fry, Esq., of New York, than whom no higher authority on such subjects can be found in this country, writes—"The history of waifs, musical and poetical, is extremely difficult to ferret out. I do not think the authorship of the air 'To Anacreon in Heaven' can be discovered. The oldest setting of words to this air that I recall is an admirable drinking song—

'When Bibo went down to the regions below,'

which I think is by Gay."

"To Anacreon in Heaven," referred to as written by Ralph Tomlinson, we copy in full from a book called the "English Musical Repository," published in London in 1807, but the words were written in England, about the year 1795, as a very close investigation has shown.

"To Anacreon in Heaven, where he sat in full glee,
    A few sons of harmony sent a petition,
That he their inspirer and patron would be;
    When this answer arrived from the jolly old Grecian:
Voice, fiddle and flute, no longer be mute,
I'll lend you my name and inspire you to boot;
And besides I'll instruct you like me to entwine,
The myrtle of Venus with Bacchus's vine.

"The news through Olympus immediately flew,
    When Old Thunder pretended to give himself airs—
If these mortals are suffered their schemes to pursue,
    The devil a goddess will stay above stairs.
Hark, already they cry, in transports of joy,
Away to the sons of Anacreon we'll fly,
And there with good fellows we'll learn to entwine
The myrtle of Venus with Bacchus's vine.

"The yellow haired god and his nine fusty maids,
    From Helicon's banks will incontinent flee,
Idalia will boast but of tenantless shades,
    And the biforked hill a mere desert will be.
My thunder no fear on't shall soon do its errand,
And d——— me! I'll swing the ringleaders I warrant,
I'll trim the young dogs for thus daring to twine
The myrtle of Venus with Bacchus's vine.

"Apollo rose up, and said, prythee ne'er quarrel,
    Good king of the gods with my votaries below;
Your thunder is useless—then showing his laurel,
    Cried, *sic evitabile fulmen*, you know,
Then over each head my laurels I'll spread,
So my sons from your crackers no mischief shall dread,

While snug in ther club-room they jovially twine
The myrtle of Venus with Bacchus's vine.

"Next Momus got up with his risible phiz,
    And swore with Apollo he'd cheerfully join—
The tide of full harmony still shall be his,
    But the song, and the catch, and the laugh shall be mine.
Then Jove be not jealous of these honest fellows;
Cried Jove, we relent, since the truth you now tell us;
And swear by old Styx, that they long shall entwine,
The myrtle of Venus with Bacchus's vine.

"Ye sons of Anacreon, then join hand in hand;
    Preserve unanimity, friendship and love;
'Tis yours to support what's so happily planned;
    You've the sanction of gods, and fiat of Jove.
While thus we agree, our toast let it be,
May our club flourish happy, united and free,
And long may the sons of Anacreon entwine,
The myrtle of Venus with Bacchus's vine."

Himself a poet, the above must have been mere gingle in the ears
of Anacreon, the great master of Bacchanalian song; and were it
not for the historical interests clustering around it, no reprint would
be found here, but our aid would be afforded to bury it forever in
the caves of the Cyclops, no more to offend the ear and corrupt the
heart of the more refined votaries of Bacchus in the present day.

With respect to this song a Kentucky correspondent of the New
York Ledger recently writes—"In the early part of the present century, 'To Anacreon in Heaven' was a favorite convivial song, and
well known. In my childhood I well remember having learned the
air from hearing a political song which was set to it, and sung with
great enthusiasm at a very large Federal dinner, given under an
immense tent on or very near to Bush Hill, in the present north-
western part of Philadelphia. It was during the administration of
Mr. Jefferson, when the struggle between Federalism and Democracy
was most severe and bitter. The title of that song, I well remember,
was, '*The Pilots whom Washington placed at the helm.*' Though a
striking composition, it has passed away with the circumstances which

called it forth, and few probably are living who remember it. Your reference to 'Anacreon in Heaven' and its authorship, brought back vividly to my mind these recollections of my boyish days, and induced me to refer to a work in my library, called the 'Universal Songster, or Museum of Mirth,' published in London in 1825, containing some thousands of songs—English, Irish, Scotch and Welch. In this work I find the old song of 'To Anacreon in Heaven' assigned to the authorship of *Ralph Tomlinson*. What else he may have done in the literary way, I know not, the name being entirely unknown to me."

The *time* when the words and the music of this song were written, as also the name of the composer of the music, remain undiscovered ; but it is quite certain that both the air and the words were unknown in America at the end of the last year of Washington's presidency. No mention is made of the song in the newspapers and popular magazines of the United States prior to 1798. In this year it was sung as *new*, and the air was first nationalized by being set to the patriotic words of the Boston song before referred to—and it is quite certain also that no national song to this air was sung at Mount Vernon prior to 1799. In this year the Boston song was sung at the home and in the hearing of the Revolutionary Chief, and it is therefore a fact that Washington, in the last year of his life, heard the soul-stirring air of

THE STAR SPANGLED BANNER

of the Second War of Independence—an air that was destined to live in the hearts of the American people as long as his fame and his country endure.

We now come to notice the invasion of Washington City by the British in 1814. On the 18th of June, 1812, the United States declared war against Great Britain, and on the 24th of August, 1814, the battle of Bladensburg was fought, which resulted the same day in the capture of Washington City by the British.

"It is our painful duty," says a writer of the day, "to place on record the melancholy fact, that the capital of the United States has fallen into the hands of the enemy ; and, what renders the circumstance the more mortifying to every American heart, by a force of only six or eight thousand men."

"On the night of the 16th, the British fleet in the Chesapeake bay, at anchor off Point Lookout, were reinforced by thirty sail of vessels, five of which were transports, making their whole force amount to fifty-one sail. On the 17th they proceeded up the bay, and a detachment of the fleet ascended the Patuxent as high as Benedict, about twenty-two miles from Washington City, where they debarked their men. About the same time, it appears another body of men were landed from another detachment of the fleet, at a point on the Potomac. On the approach of the enemy, Com. Barney ordered his flotilla to be blown up, to prevent its falling into their hands. Our troops under Gen. Winder, advanced towards the enemy as far as Bladensburg, six miles from Washington, at which place a severe engagement took place."

"Upon the approach of the enemy, our artillery and infantry opened upon them with briskness, and did considerable execution, as numbers of them were seen to fall. The enemy marched steadily forward in close column, apparently disregarding the fire, and reserving their own, until our troops began to retreat, when they let drive at them. Our troops not being one-quarter equal to the enemy in number, received orders to retire, and fled in all directions, and the enemy pursued their course to Washington. Com. Barney, with his gallant flotilla crew, bravely disputed the entrance of the enemy into the city. The Baltimore troops, in the first instance, bore the brunt of the battle, and behaved with the utmost coolness and courage. Twice they bore so hard on the enemy as to stagger his progress. Gen. Stansbury, Com. Barney, Maj. Pinckney and Capt. Sterrett, are among the wounded ; the brave Commodore very severely. The President of the United States, the Secretary of State, and the Secretary of War, were in view of the enemy when they advanced. The Navy Yard, frigate Essex, and the sloop of war Argus, were burnt by our own troops previous to the enemy's arrival in the city. The enemy destroyed the capitol, the President's House, and all the other public buildings, except the Post Office, which they mistook for a private dwelling. A house belonging to Mr. Gallatin, and several others, were destroyed, in consequence of some men being secreted in them, who fired on the enemy and shot the horse from under Gen. Ross."

"Having thus succeeded in his attack on Washington, the elated enemy directed his attention towards Baltimore, and began immediately to concentrate the various detachments of his fleet, and make arrangements for an attack on that city. The fleet destined against Baltimore consisted of nearly forty sail, several of them ships of the line, and on their approach to the mouth of the Patapsco, the alarm was promptly spread through the city and the adjoining country. The largest vessels anchored across the channel, and the troops intended for the land attack were debarked upon North Point, fourteen miles distant from the city by land, and about twelve by water. On the morning of September 12, 1814, between seven and eight thousand soldiers, sailors, and marines, had effected a landing, while sixteen bomb vessels and frigates proceeded up the river, and anchored within two miles and a half of Fort McHenry."

"General Stricker," says Maj. Gen. Smith, "had been detached on Sunday evening with a portion of his brigade on the North Point road. Major Randall, of the Baltimore county militia, having under his command a light corps of riflemen and musketry, taken from Gen. Stansbury's brigade and the Pennsylvania volunteers, was detached to the mouth of Bear Creek, with orders to co-operate with Gen. Stricker, and to check any landing which the enemy might attempt to make in that quarter. On Monday Gen. Stricker took a good position at the two roads leading from the city to North Point, having his right flanked by Bear Creek, and his left by a marsh. He here awaited the approach of the enemy, having sent on an advance corps under the command of Major Heath, of the fifth regiment. This advance was met by that of the enemy, and after some skirmishing it returned to the line, the main body of the enemy being at a short distance in the rear of their advance. Between two and three o'clock, the enemy's whole force came up and commenced the battle by some discharges of rockets, which were succeeded by the cannon from both sides, and soon after the action became general along the line. Gen. Stricker gallantly maintained his ground against a great superiority of numbers during the space of an hour and twenty minutes, when the regiment on his left giving way, he was under the necessity of retiring to the ground in his rear, where he had stationed one regiment as a reserve. He here formed his brigade; but the enemy not thinking it advisable to pursue, he, in compliance with previous arrangements, fell back and
9*

took post on the left of our entrenchments, and a half mile in advance of them. In this affair the citizen soldiers of Baltimore, with the exception of the fifty-first regiment, have maintained the reputation they so deservedly acquired at Bladensburg, and their brave and skillful leader has confirmed the confidence which we all had so justly placed in him."

"About the time Gen. Stricker had taken the ground just mentioned, he was joined by Gen. Winder, who had been stationed on the west side of the city, but was now ordered to march with Gen. Douglass's brigade of Virginia militia and United States dragoons, under Capt. Baird, and take post on the left of Gen. Stricker. During these movements, the brigades of Generals Stansbury and Foreman, the seamen and marines under Commodore Rogers, the Pennsylvania volunteers under Colonels Cobean and Findley, the Baltimore artillery under Capt. Stiles, manned the trenches and the batteries—all prepared to receive the enemy. We remained in this situation during the night."

"On Tuesday the enemy appeared in front of our entrenchments, at the distance of two miles on the Philadelphia road, from whence he had a full view of our position. He manœuvred during the morning towards our left, as if with the intention of making a circuitous march and coming down on the Harford or York road. Generals Winder and Stricker were ordered to adapt their movements to those of the enemy, so as to baffle his supposed intention. They executed this order with great skill and judgment, by taking an advantageous position, stretching from our left across the country, when the enemy was likely to approach the quarter he seemed to threaten. This movement induced the enemy to concentrate his forces in our front, pushing his advance to within a mile of us, driving in our videttes, and showing an intention of attacking us that evening. I immediately drew Generals Winder and Stricker nearer to the left of my entrenchments and to the right of the enemy, with the intention of their falling on his right or rear, should he attack me; or, if he declined it, of attacking him in the morning. To this movement and to the strength of my defences, which the enemy had the fairest opportunity of observing, I am induced to attribute his retreat, which was commenced at half-past one o'clock on Wednesday morning. In this he was so favored by the extreme darkness and a continued rain, that we did not discover it until day-light. I consented to Gen. Winder pursuing with the Virginia brigade and the United States dragoons; at the same time Maj. Randall was dispatched with his light corps in pursuit of the enemy's right, whilst the whole of the militia cavalry was put in motion for the same object. All the troops were, however, so worn out with continued watching, and with being under arms during three days and nights, exposed the greater part of the time to very inclement weather, that it was found impracticable to do any thing more than to pick up a few stragglers. The enemy commenced his embarkation that evening, and completed it the next day at one o'clock."

"On Tuesday morning, about sunrise," says Col. Armistead, who commanded in Fort McHenry, "the enemy commenced the attack from his five bomb vessels, at the distance of about two miles, when, finding that the shells reached us, he anchored, and kept up an incessant and well-directed bombardment. We immediately opened our batteries, and kept up a brisk fire from our guns and mortars; but, unfortunately, all our shot and shells fell considerably short of him. This was to me a most distressing circumstance, as it left us exposed to a constant and tremendous shower of shells, without the most remote possibility of doing him the slightest injury. It affords me the highest gratification to state that, though we were left thus exposed and thus inactive, not a man shrunk from the conflict. About two o'clock, P. M., one of the twenty-four-pounders of the southwest bastion, under the immediate command of Capt. Nicholson, was dismounted by a shell, the explosion from which killed his second lieutenant, and wounded several of his men; the bustle necessarily produced in removing the wounded and replacing the gun, probably induced the enemy to suspect we were in a state of confusion, as he brought in three of his bomb-ships to what I believed to be a good striking distance. I immediately ordered a fire to be opened, which was obeyed with alacrity through the whole garrison, and in half an hour these intruders again sheltered themselves by withdrawing beyond our reach. We gave three cheers, and again ceased firing. The enemy continued throwing shells, with one or two slight intermissions, till one o'clock on the morning of Wednesday, when it was discovered he had availed himself of the darkness of the night, and had thrown a considerable force above to our right;

they had approached very near to Fort Covington, when they began to throw rockets; intended, I presume, to give them an opportunity of examining the shores. As I have since understood, they had detached twelve hundred and fifty picked men, with scaling ladders, for the purpose of storming this fort. We once more had an opportunity of opening our batteries, and kept up a continued blaze for near two hours, which had the effect again to drive them off.

"In justice to Lieutenant Newcomb, of the United States Navy, who commanded at Fort Covington with a detachment of sailors, and Lieutenant Webster, of the flotilla, who commanded the six-gun battery near that fort, I ought to state that, during this time, they kept up an animated, and, 1 believe, a very destructive fire, to which, I am persuaded, we are much indebted in repulsing the enemy. The only means we had of directing our guns was by the blaze of their rockets, and the flashes of their guns. The bombardment continued on the part of the enemy until seven o'clock on Wednesday morning, when it ceased; and about nine their ships got under weigh and stood down the river. During the bombardment, which lasted twenty-five hours, from the best calculation I can make, from fifteen to eighteen hundred shells were thrown by the enemy. A few of these fell short. A large portion burst over us, throwing their fragments among us, and threatening destruction. Many passed over, and about four hundred fell within the works."

In just such awfully sublime and terrific blazes of death, and nowhere else, when victory, amid mingled shouts of triumph, has perched upon the national banner, the dormant inspiration of a people, ensconced somewhere tarrying for the circumstances of its birth, often breaks forth in song! Some accurate thinker has said, "Let me write a nation's songs, and 1 care not who makes its laws." Long had slept the American bard. The thunders of the French war cloud of '98 awoke him to glory in the person of Joseph Hopkinson. For sixteen years he slept again, and then awoke by the "rocket's red glare," in the person of Francis S. Key, a prisoner on board a British transport, in American waters, in 1814!

"A gentleman had left Baltimore with a flag of truce," says a cotemporaneous writer, "for the purpose of getting released from the British fleet a friend of his, who had been captured at Marlborough. He went as far as the mouth of the Patuxent, and was not permitted to return, lest the intended attack on Baltimore should be disclosed. He was therefore brought up the bay to the mouth of the Patapsco, where the flag-vessel was kept under the guns of a frigate, and he was compelled to witness the bombardment of Fort McHenry, which the Admiral had boasted he would carry in a few hours, and that the city must fall. He watched the flag at the fort through the whole day, with an anxiety that can be more easily conceived than described, until the night prevented him from seeing it. In the night he watched the bomb shells, and at early dawn his eye was again greeted by the proudly waving flag of his country."

On board the transport, through the whole day, and the perilous night succeeding, the genius of inspiration stood by Mr. Key, guiding his thoughts and his pencil; while to the air "Anacreon in Heaven," he penciled a poem; and when the haughty foe no longer reposed in dread silence on freedom's shore, he was released from the transport and repaired to the house of Judge Nicholson, in the city, and there gave form to his immortal

"STAR-SPANGLED BANNER."

Such patriotic emotions as now visited the bosom of Mr. Key were too restless to be confined there; too exhilirating to find utterance in ordinary language, and too sublime to find birth except in the most chaste expression and glowing imagery. From the transport he had gazed with admiration on the silent heavens as displaying the glory of God; and from instantaneous impulse, acting upon a mind well stored with abundant materials, treasured up for some occasion that might bring them into use, he framed the Star-Spangled Banner, the pride and glory of every American heart. The fire which burns through his poem was not elaborated spark by spark from mechanical friction; but it was in the open air, under the cope of heaven, that our second national Franklin caught his lightnings from the cloud of thought as it passed over him, and communicated them, too, by a touch, with electrical swiftness, amid the inspiration of the thunder of the bursting bomb, and the lightning of the glaring rocket.

On the authority of Mr. John S. Skinner, of Baltimore, Capt. A. H. Kilty, of the United States Navy, pens an able communication to the writer on this subject, from which the following extracts are made:

"The British, while on their retreat from Washington," says Capt. Kilty, "had seized upon several gentlemen of Prince George's, among whom were Gov. Bowie and a Mr. Beans, and it was to obtain their release that Mr. Key, under a flag of truce, and accompanied by Mr. John S. Skinner, of Baltimore, visited the fleet. The attack on Baltimore was then in contemplation ; and lest intelligence of the fact should transpire through Mr. Key or his companion, it was considered expedient to detain them with the fleet ; and it was not therefore until after the repulse of the British that they were liberated. On landing in or near Baltimore, they proceeded at once to the residence of Judge Nicholson, Mr. Key's brother-in-law, who had shared in the defence of Fort McHenry, and there it was that the 'Star-Spangled Banner' was prepared for the press. Its appearance in the public papers was hailed with a degree of enthusiasm which knew no abatement until the outbreak of the rebellion now devastating the land ; but the song, nevertheless, will live in the hearts of the loyal as long as we are a nation.

"The house of Judge Nicholson was in Market street, near the corner of Eutaw, and next to the one occupied for many subsequent years by Mr. Solomon Etting."

But, returning to the British transport, that loathsome prison-house for a freeman, we behold the genius of inspiration ministering to the towering soul of the immortal Key ; and, gazing at the picture illumined by the glare of the rocket piercing the skies, and the fatal bomb breaking the solitudes of night, we are fanned to a blaze of enthusiasm that burns in classic thought.

> "Thou hast seen Mount Athos ;
> While storms and tempests thunder at its brow
> And oceans beat their billows at its feet,
> It stands unmoved and glories in its height,
> Such is that mighty man ; his towering soul
> 'Mid all the shocks and injuries of fortune,
> Rises superior and looks down on Cæsar."

And such is our own American Key, who is next seen to dip his pencil in the light of heaven, and wresting the air from old England as our Conscript Fathers wrested Yankee Doodle, he traced immortal characters before us, nationalized the air, and engraved a nation's song as in eternal brass to shine forever, singing as he wrote—

O! say, can you see, by the dawn's early light,
　What so proudly we hailed at the twilight's last gleaming,
Whose broad stripes and bright stars through the perilous fight,
　O'er the ramparts we watched were so gallantly streaming?
And the rockets' red glare, the bombs bursting in air,
Gave proof through the night that our flag was still there;
　　O! say, does that star-spangled banner yet wave,
　　O'er the land of the free, and the home of the brave?

On the shore dimly seen through the mists of the deep,
　Where the foe's haughty host in dread silence reposes,
What is that which the breeze, o'er the towering steep,
　As it fitfully blows, half conceals, half discloses?
Now it catches the gleam of the morning's first beam,
In full glory reflected now shines on the stream;
　　'Tis the star-spangled banner, O! long may it wave
　　O'er the land of the free, and the home of the brave.

And where is that band who so vauntingly swore
　That the havoc of war and the battle's confusion,
A home and a country should leave us no more?
　Their blood has washed out their foul footsteps' pollution.
No refuge could save the hireling and slave,
From the terror of flight and the gloom of the grave.
　　And the star-spangled banner in triumph doth wave,
　　O'er the land of the free, and the home of the brave.

O! thus be it ever when freemen shall stand
　Between their loved home, and the war's desolation,
Blest with victory and peace may the heaven-rescued land,
　Praise the Power that hath made and preserved us a nation!
Then conquer we must, when our cause it is just,
And this be our motto—"In God is our trust."
　　And the star-spangled banner in triumph shall wave,
　　O'er the land of the free and the home of the brave.

"Capt. Benjamin Edes, who commanded a company at the battle of North Point, printed the "Star-Spangled Banner" at his office, on the corner of Baltimore and Gay streets, and scattered it broadcast, on a single slip, throughout the saved city. It was everywhere sung with loud applause; and the prowess of Col. Armistead and his little band in defending Fort McHenry, was a theme for praise upon every lip."

Old Defenders of Baltimore! say can you still see, with the dim eye of age, that illustrious spot where you battled for freedom, and where the foe's haughty host in dread silence reposed on the shores of Maryland? If you still see that spot where your brothers' bones repose, does not your patriotism gain force, and your piety grow warmer when you contemplate your "heaven-rescued land?" Has the lapse of half a century cooled your hearts and rendered your flag less lovely? Is not your flag lovelier now than then? Visit North Point once more that the past may predominate over the present. "Far from me and from my friends," says Dr. Johnson, quoting him once more, "be such frigid philosophy as may conduct us, indifferent and unmoved, over any ground which has been dignified by wisdom, bravery or virtue. That man is little to be envied whose patriotism would not gain force on the plain of Marathon, or whose piety would not grow warmer among the ruins of Iona."

While you stand upon the last promontory of life, with more than half a century of years behind, and the great eternal ocean before you, will you not with me, in place of Marathon, substitute North Point, Fort McHenry, the Lazaretto, the six-gun battery, and Fort Covington?

"Yankee Doodle Dandy," which the Fathers of the Republic wrested from the foe at Concord and Lexington in '75, the "Hail Columbia" of our Washington, and your own "Star-Spangled Banner," whose air was wrested from the same foe in 1814, have been recently cast into the crucible, the spirit flame kindled, and the compound blow-pipe of treason applied, but they are destined to come forth from their intense heat without the smell of fire upon them, and live forever.

"The appearance of the Star-Spangled Banner in the public papers of 1814," says Capt. Kilty, "was hailed with a degree of enthusiasm which knew no abatement until the outbreak now devastating our land." This has been strictly true in every nation under heaven that has heard the American name and the Star-Spangled Banner; and in no Trans-Atlantic country has the words or the air ever been assailed in public, except as in the following instance—the account we clip from the Liverpool Post of October 1, 1863. "The Americans carry their patriotic prejudices into the concert room. A few nights since, at Scarborough, Mrs. Howard Paul, while singing the Star-Spangled Banner, the national lyric of the United States, was assailed with a storm of hisses by a party of Southern Americans, who are sojourning at that watering place. One of the local journals, in commenting upon the affair, explains that Mrs. Howard Paul had not the slightest political motive in singing the lyric, but simply inserted it in her programme as a beautiful melody, which possessed an additional interest from its being an old English air, adopted and nationalized on the other side of the Atlantic." Americans ! !

"Every people becomes imbued, steeped as it were, in the fervor, the inspiration, the fire of their bards. All great nations have become thrilled and moved to perform noble and heroic deeds by the rich melodies of their songsters. Every ordeal under which a nation moves, through strife or war, tends, like the subject which passes through the crucible, to make it more pure, more bright, and more powerful.

"By contention, by friction, by abrasion, all the powers of human ingenuity become exerted, and invention and construction in multitudinous forms, is the result. No nation has ever surpassed this in these powers. The poet, among the rest, has winged his soul towards heaven, and, basking in the sun-light there, has daguerreotyped his feelings into poetry and transmitted them into song. These feelings, thoughts, and instincts, will live forever. The nation which fails to transmit ennobling song to its posterity, thereby writes its own epitaph—it sounds its own death-knell from the belfry above, whilst the church below is all on fire."

"Wouldst thou know," says Confucius, "if a people be well governed, if its manners be good, examine the music it practices."

"When I play upon my *king*," says Kouie, a Chinese musician, "the animals range themselves spell-bound before me with melody."

The skill with which Orpheus struck the lyre was fabled to have been such as to move the very trees and rocks, and the beasts of the forests assembled around him as he touched its chords. Armed with his lyre he entered the realms of Hades, and gained an easy admittance to the palace of Pluto. At the music of his golden shell, to borrow the beautiful language of ancient poetry, the wheel of

10

Ixion ceased to revolve, Tantalus forgot the thirst that tormented him, and the inhabitants of that dark despair were for a season refreshed by the dew-laden balmy notes of music.

Sing on then, bards of America! engrave your national melodies on every heart; then purple mountains of fame, like Alps on Alps, will loom up before you—and as long as a nation lives on this continent, consecrated by the foot-prints of Washington, may the melodies of Yankee Doodle Dandy, Hail Columbia, and the Star-Spangled Banner, never cease to refresh the heart of every nation of the world, nor fail to rally the noble sons of freedom to the American standard.

Hail! Sovereign of the world of flags! whose majesty and might
First dazzles, then enraptures, then overawes the sight;
The shining kings and emperors in every clime and zone,
Grow dim before thy stars and sit uneasy on the throne.

No fleets can stop thy progress, no armies bid thee stay,
But onward, onward, onward thy march still holds its way;
The rising dust that veils thee as thine herald, goes before,
And the music that proclaims thee is the booming cannon's roar.

The sun, the moon, and all the orbs that shine upon thee now,
Beheld the wreath of glory which first bound thy infant brow;
Thy reign is of the ancient days, thy birth is from on high,
Just where Great Washington, our star, first lit Columbia's sky.
  We'll rally round the stars and stripes until the victory's won,
  Or perish in their light to save the chair of Washington.

CHAPTER VIII.

In 1799 we left Mount Vernon with solemn reflections, on account
of the pall of gloom that was about to darken the bright skies of
autumn there; for on the 14th of December, in that year, it was
announced that "Washington is no more."

"These are my Wills," said he, just before he died. "Preserve this
and burn the other."

"The designated will was burned."

"The group gathered near to the couch of the sufferer, watching
with intense anxiety for the slightest dawning of hope."

"I am very ill," he said in reply to an affectionate old servant that
smoothed down his pillow.

"I am dying, sir, but am not afraid to die," said he to Dr. Craik.

"I find I am going :" said he, "my breath cannot last long; I believed from the first that my disorder would prove fatal. Arrange
my accounts and settle my books."

"Let Mr. Rawlins finish recording my other letters which he has
begun."

"I am certainly near my end," said the dying chief. "It is a
debt we all must pay. I look to the event with perfect resignation."

"I am afraid I fatigue you too much," the General would say.

"Christopher, sit down," said he to his faithful body-servant, who
had been standing by him all day.

"Doctor, I die hard, but I am not afraid to go," said he, turning
his eyes on Dr. Craik.

"How long am I to remain in this situation ?" he inquired.

"Not long sir," replied the doctor.

"I feel I am going," said Washington, "I thank you for your attentions, but I pray you to take no more trouble about me. Let me go off quietly."

"He took whatever was offered him."

"I am just going," said he, "have me decently buried, and do not let my body be put into the vault in less than three days after I am dead."

"Do you understand me ?" he inquired. "I replied, yes."

"'Tis well," said he.

"He felt his own pulse. I saw his countenance change. His hand fell from his wrist—I took it in mine."

"Is he gone ?" inquired Mrs. Washington.

"I held up my hand as a signal that he was no more."

"'Tis well," said she, "I shall soon follow him. I have no more trials to pass through."

"Tears chased each other down the furrowed cheeks of Dr. Craik."

"Mrs. Washington was seen kneeling at the bed side, her head resting upon her Bible, which had been her solace in the many and heavy afflictions she had undergone. She could with difficulty be removed from the chamber of death."

"Yesterday," writes an eye-witness, "I attended the funeral of the saviour of our country at Mount Vernon ; and had the honor of being one who carried his body to the vault. He was borne by military gentlemen, and brethren of our lodge, of which he was formerly Master. To describe the scene is impossible. The coffin bore his sword and apron ; the members of the lodge walked as mourners, his horse was led, properly caparisoned, by two of his servants in mourning."

"As I helped to place his body in the vault, and stood at the door while the funeral service was performing, I had the best opportunity of observing the countenances of all. Every one was affected, but none so much as *his colored domestics of all ages.*"

"The sun was now sitting ! Alas ! the sun of glory was set forever ! ! No—the name of Washington, the American President and General, will triumph over death ! The unclouded brightness of his glory will illume future ages !"

"When the burst of grief which followed the death of the Pater Patriæ had a little subsided, visits of condolence to the bereaved lady were made by the first personages of the land."

"Although the great sun of attraction had sunk in the west, still the radiance shed by his illustrious life and actions drew crowds of pilgrims to his tomb. The establishment of Mount Vernon was kept up to its former standard, and the lady presided with her wonted ease and dignity of manner, at her hospitable board. She relaxed not in her attentions to her domestic concerns, performing the arduous duties of the mistress of so extensive an establishment, although in the 69th year of her age, and evidently suffering in her spirits from the heavy bereavement she had so lately sustained."

"Upon the decease of my wife," wrote the General in his will, "it is my will and desire, that all the slaves which I hold in *my' own right*, shall receive their freedom. To emancipate them during her life, would, though earnestly wished by me, be attended by such insuperable difficulties on account of their intermixture with the dower negroes, as to excite the most painful sensation, if not disagreeable consequences to the latter, while both descriptions are in the occupancy of the same proprietor, it not being in my power, under the tenure by which the dower negroes are held, to manumit them. And whereas, among those who will receive freedom according to this devise, there may be some who, from old age or bodily infirmities, and others, who on account of their infancy, will be unable to support themselves, it is my will and desire, that all who come under the first and second descriptions, shall be comfortably clothed and fed by my heirs while they live; and that such of the latter description as have no parents living, or, if living are unable or unwilling to provide for them, shall be bound by the court until they shall arrive at the age of twenty-five years; and in cases where no record can be produced whereby their ages can be ascertained, the judgment of the court, upon its own view of the subject, shall be adequate and final. The negroes thus bound are, by their masters and mistresses, to be taught to read and write, and be brought up to some useful occupation, agreeably to the laws of the commonwealth of Virginia providing for the support of orphan and other poor children. And I do hereby expressly forbid the sale or transportation out of the said Commonwealth of any slave I may

10*

die possessed of, under any pretense whatever. And I do moreover most pointedly and most solemnly enjoin upon my executors hereaf-- ter named, or the survivor of them, to see that *this* clause respecting slaves, and every part thereof, be religiously fulfilled at the epoch at which it is desired to take place, without evasion, neglect, or delay, after the crops which may be then on the ground are harvested, particularly, as it respects the aged and infirm ; seeing that a regular and permanent fund be established for their support, as long as there are subjects requiring it, not trusting to the uncertain provisions made by individuals. And to my mulatto man William, calling himself William Lee, I give immediate freedom, or, if he should prefer it, on account of the accidents which have befallen him, and which have rendered him incapable of walking, or of any active employment, to remain in the situation he now is, it shall be optional in him to do so ; in either case however, I allow him an annuity of thirty dollars during his natural life, which shall be independent of the victuals and clothes he has been accustomed to receive, if he chooses the latter alternative; but in full with his freedom, if he prefers the first, and this I give him as a testimony of my sense of attachment to me, and for his faithful services during the revolutionary war."

"The whole number of negroes left by General Washington, in his own right, is as follows : Forty men, thirty-seven women, four working boys, three working girls, and forty children, making in all *one hundred and twenty-four.*"

"The slaves were left to be emancipated at the death of Mrs. Washington, but it was found necessary, *for prudential reasons*, to give them their freedom in one year after the General's decease. Although many of them, with a view to their liberation, had been instructed in mechanical trades, yet they succeeded very badly as freemen, so true is the axiom that, *the hour which makes man a slave, takes half his worth away.*"

"A little more than two years from the demise of the Chief, Mrs. Washington became alarmingly ill from an attack of bilious fever. From her advanced age, the sorrow that had preyed upon her spirits, and the severity of the attack, the family physician gave but little hope of a favorable issue. The lady herself was perfectly aware that her hour was nigh ; she assembled her grand-children at her bed side, discoursed to them on their respective duties through life, spoke of the happy influences of religion on the affairs of this world, of the consolations they had afforded her in many and trying afflictions; and of the hopes they held out of a blessed immortality; and then surrounded by her weeping relatives, friends and domestics, the venerable relic of Washington resigned her life into the hands of her Creator, in the 71st year of her age."

The papers of the day published the following notice of her death: "Died at Mount Vernon, on Saturday evening, the 22d of May, 1802, Mrs. Martha Washington, widow of the late illustrious General George Washington. To those amiable and christian virtues which adorn the female character, she added dignity of manners, superiority of understanding, a mind intelligent and elevated. The silence of respectful grief is our best eulogy."

After bequeathing her principal property to her different relatives, the following sentence appears in her will: "It is my will and desire that all the rest and residue of my estate, of whatever kind and description, not herein specifically devised or bequeathed, shall be sold by the executors of this my last will, for ready money." This clause included all the dower negroes of Mrs. Washington, referred to in the will of the General, as having intermarried with those in his own right. The dower negroes were now, by will, to be sold as slaves for life, and our young turkey driver being one of the number, soon found a good master in the person of Washington's old friend, Dr. Craik, of Alexandria.

Washington's servants were all free—Mrs. Washington's all slaves. Sorrow took the place of cheerfulness and joy, and Mount Vernon's groves no longer heard the happy songs of the days of the Chief. Immense estates, mountains, and rivers soon rolled between the two classes of negroes—the Mount became sad, and its groves a tuneless wild.

In 1802, the old family vault now contained all that was earthly of the beloved chief, and Martha, his wife. Within these walls no echoing sound had disturbed the "strangely solemn peace" for more than a quarter of a century after the interment; and no "curious fool" had attempted to "pry on corruption." Death reigned alone, and "the fearful mysteries of change were being there enacted."

The building of the new tomb, "at the foot of what is called the

Vineyard enclosure," was delayed for many years, and, in the meantime, the "curious fool" began his work on the old one ; and now on a page of American history it is written—"the construction of this tomb was delayed until many years ago, when an attempt was made to carry off the remains of the illustrious dead ! The old vault was entered, and a skull and some bones were taken away. They formed no part of the remains of Washington. The robbers were detected, and the bones were recovered."

In October, 1837, there was a gathering before the tomb of Washington on an interesting occasion. This was for the re-entombing of Washington and his wife. "Mr. John Struthers, of Philadelphia, generously offered to present two marble coffins in which the remains of the patriot and his consort might he placed for preservation forever, for already the wooden coffins, which covered the leaden ones containing their ashes, had been three times renewed."

"On Saturday, the 7th of October, 1837, Mr. Strickland, of Philadelphia, accompanied by a number of the Washington family, assisted in placing the remains of the illustrious dead in the receptacles where they have ever since been undisturbed."

"The vault was first entered by Mr. Strickland, accompanied by Major Lewis."

On entering the vault, "they found everything in confusion. Decayed fragments of coffins were scattered about, and bones of various parts of the human body were seen promiscuously thrown together. The decayed wood was dripping with moisture. The slimy snail glistened in the light of the door opening. The brown centipede was disturbed by the admission of fresh air, and the mouldy cases of the dead gave out a pungent and unwholesome odor. The coffins of Washington and his lady were in the deepest recess of the vault. They were of lead, enclosed in wooden cases. When the sarcophagus arrived, the coffin of the chief was brought forth. When the decayed wooden case was removed, the leaden lid was perceived to be sunken and fractured. In the bottom of the wooden case was found the silver coffin-plate, in the form of a shield, which was placed upon the leaden coffin when Washington was first entombed. At the request of Mr. Lewis, the fractured part of the lid was turned over on the lower part, exposing to view a head and breast of large dimensions, which appeared, by the dim light of the candles, to have suffered but little from the effects of time. The eye-sockets were large and deep, and the breadth across the temples, together with the forehead, appeared of unusual size. There was no appearance of grave-clothes; the chest was broad, the color was dark, and had the appearance of dried flesh, and skin adhering closely to the bones. We saw no hair, nor was there any offensive odor from the body, but we observed, when the coffin had been removed to the outside of the vault, the dripping down of a yellow liquid, which stained the marble of the sarcophagus. A hand was laid upon the head, and instantly removed; the leaden lid was restored to its place; the body, raised by six men, was carried and laid in the marble coffin, and the ponderous cover being put on and set in cement, it was sealed from our sight."

"The remains of Mrs. Washington being placed in the other marble sarcophagus, they were both boxed so as to prevent their being injured during the finishing of the vestibule of the new vault in its present form."

"The relatives who were present, consisting of Major Lewis, Lorenzo Lewis, John Augustine Washington, George Washington, the Rev. Mr. Johnson and lady, and Mrs. Jane Washington, then retired to the mansion."

"O, death, what art thou?—nurse of dreamless slumbers freshening the fevered flesh to a wakefulness eternal—strange and solemn alchemist, elaborating life's elixir from these clayey crucibles?"

Let us next pause to inquire of "Father Jack," the old fisherman. The spring of 1800 numbers him with the dead of the great past.

"Poor Father Jack! No more at early dawn will he be seen as, with withered arms, he paddled his light canoe on the broad surface of the Potomac, to return with the finny spoils, and boast of famous fish taken on his own hook. His canoe has long since rotted on the shore; his paddle hangs idle in his cabin; his occupation's gone, and Father Jack, the old fisherman of Mount Vernon, sleeps the sleep that knows no waking."

"I approached the spot where the cold moon looked down from a pure blue heaven, forming dark shadows from innumerable grave-stones. The solemn stillness of death reigned there, and I almost became petrified by sympathy as I gazed upon this dilapidated city of the dead. The chisel of time was swiftly touching down to dust every memorial of the venerable dead; but I soon discovered the spot where rests the ashes of poor old John Tasker, the aged fisherman of Mount Vernon, who, for many long years, had supplied the tables at the mansion of Washington with the choicest fish of the season. After looking intently for the last time on his humble resting-place, I rode briskly, facing the cold breeze, until I reached the mansion of the Chief."

Little Jack, the leader of the choir, Aunt Dolly, Aunt Phillis, Cully, Jr., poor old Bristol, and Mose, the cow-boy, found a home among the Lees; but Scomberry, the philosopher of Dogue Run, remained at his little home in Green Willow Hollow, and was provided for as stated in Washington's will.

From the death of Mrs. Washington in 1802, there was now and then a death, a marriage, and a departure from the Mount, thinning the ranks of servants there, both old and young, until Scomberry was left alone in Green Willow Hollow—the patriarch of the Mount.

Nothing occurred to rouse the old hermit from his solitude, or move him to speak in prophecy, until Aaron Burr went down the Ohio river in 1805. In the spring of 1806, Burr's treason began to be whispered in the ear, but before the close of autumn it was proclaimed from the house tops. The sound of treason at that early day in the history of the government, startled the patriarch of Mount Vernon, and prompted him to speak once more in the voice of prophecy; warning his countrymen of the danger that threatened the land of Washington, and describing the characters that would sympathize with Burr and his disciples in treason.

With Billy Lee, and the remnant of old servants of '98, still lingering around the Mount in 1806, as an audience, Scomberry proceeded to speak in prophecy as follows:

"De traitor gwine to seek, sar, to sell dis country dear,
    And trade it back to red-coats jes for a keg o' beer;
    But soon we's gwine to neck him, or send him to adorn
    De cock-loft ob de parlyment, wid tarkeys all done gone.
    Now all de future traitors like Cataline will fight,
    And, like de 'famous Arnold am gwine to swear dar right,

Den up will spring de army all out in battle drawn,
And down will go de traitor, *wid tarkeys all done gone.*
He's gwine to smell de powder, dat villainous compound,
What blowed up Tommy Davis, likewise blowed up de groun
And hit his nasal 'boscis a hard and 'founded blow,
Dat sumpin jes did *happen*, he had the signs to know.
Now way down in de futur Ise bored a 'normous hole,
And plowed de ground o' science jes like de no-eyed mole;
I sees right froo de hist'ry jes like I sees dat lawn,
And spies de futur Arnold, *wid tarkeys all done gone.*
I sees de *polly*-tician wid trick, and cheat, and lie,
Too proud to live by labor, and yet not fit to die;
He's gwine to be too lazy to follow up his trade,
Or work his weedy 'taters by usin' ob de spade;
Wid not a speck o' larnin', but bred at de cross roads,
He'll 'tempt to 'struct de people, and write de nation's codes,
He'll say Ise jes discubbered dis country's in de dark,
And when he comes to writin' he'll sign his name by mark;
And 'spound de constitution, and babble to confound
De wise and 'gacious statesmen what may be standin' round,
And wisely say, O people, I knows what Ise about,
For Washington was dreamin', I'll let de secret out—
His government's a failure, I knows it, so I does,
I see its not so lastin' our fathers guessed it was;
We's picked it, and we's robbed it, and stolen all de gold,
And find de constitution am growin' weak and old,
Our fathers jes intended dat we should tar it up,
And made it for dat reason jes like a cracky cup;
He whistles for de robbers! and rabble ob de town,
Now charge, says he, brave rabble! we'll pull dis country down,
It wont require much fightin', Ise wise, and jes can tell,
But, for you, my brave rabble, its jes a breakfus spell;
But soon dat 'bloated 'ramus will wake up late some morn,
And spy all round and hollow, *my tarkeys all done gone.*
Den round he'll spy for satellites, for catspaws and for tools,
He'll nebber want for rascals but may be scarce o' fools;
De turnspit and de scullion, and he what dribe de dray;
And he what burn de coal-pit, and he what scrape de tray:

And he what dribe de oxen, and he what dribe de mule ;
And ebry ignoramus jes neber sont to school,
And he what make de mortar, and he what toat de hod,
And he what act de cobbler, and he what hop de clod :
And he what shuck de oyster, and he what fish de crab ;
And he what sweep de chimney, and he what live by gab :
And she what wash de dishes, and she what milk de cow ;
And she what walk de city, and live I can't say how ;
And she what lives in Main street, wid parlor jes complete :
Wid one ole greasy nigger, and nuffin 'tall to eat ;
And she what keeps de lap-dog, and one, two, free, four curs :
And sells de back-room furniture to buy a set o' furs ;
And all de half-inch rustycrats what's 'normous hard to beat,
Dat spy all round de hotel to see who's gwine to treat—
Am gwine all ob a sudden to 'come so mighty wise,
And always keep wide open de trap what catch de flies ;
To 'spound de constitution and babble 'bout dar rights,
And strut 'bout 'mong de upper crust and all de lesser lights,
And nebber blush at treason, but always blushed before,
When readin' 'bout de little fly what left at de back door.
De persins numerated will babble 'bout dar rights,
And drink de wine o' treason, and 'dulge in dreamy flights.
Yes, sar, says a bold dreamer, I'll jump right off dis cart,
And 'lectioneer for Congress—right in Ise gwine to dart !
Ise jes now seed a thing sar, I nebber seed before,
O Ise a man o' talents ! I'll dribe dis cart no more.
Up jumps his wife a smilin', and frows her patchin' down,
And darts up stairs like lightnin', to get her Sunday gown ;
And dodges froo de alley, and comes to Market street,
And promenades de city to see who she can meet.
She soon meets Mrs. Uppercrust, wid traitor colors on,
Who tells 'bout a new government we'll hab as sure's you born.
Dear madam, whar's your husband ? says she, I hopes he's right,
And for dis new, great government is willing now to fight ?
He's gone, says Mrs. Stitchlouse, wid all his soul and heart,
Jes look right in dat coal-yard—dar stands his idle cart !
Ise glad, says Mrs. Uppercrust—my husband's gone to court,
But 'bout de hour o' midnight, he's gwine to seize dat Fort !

And den he's gwine to Congress to live in mighty style,
Den I'll be Mrs. Congressman, and scorn dis Union vile.
But soon she spies a risin', a 'normous cloud o' dust,
For gracious sake what am dat ? says she, my heart will bust,
O dat's dis country's army, my glory's at an end,
I'll go in dat dark garret, for I has got no friend.
Den shouts de ignoramus, what made you fool me so !
Dat mighty Union army am gwine to Mexico ;
It has jes 'bout a million ! jes hear dat bugle horn !
You's kotch me in a gull trap ! *my larkeys all done gone !*

In the spring of 1807, Scomberry found a peaceful grave beside
his old friend, the venerable fisherman of the Mount. His prophecy
was not fulfilled in the life and times of Aaron Burr ; but all his
types and shadows found an interpretation after the lapse of half a
century, as the following notice of Mount Vernon will show—

"It has been the prayer of every patriot," writes the Lieutenant
General of the United States, a half century after Scomberry's prophecy was uttered, "that the tramp and din of civil war might at
least spare the precincts within which repose the sacred remains of
the Father of his country ; but this pious hope is disappointed.
Mount Vernon, so recently consecrated anew to the Immortal Washington by the Ladies of America, has already been overrun by bands
of rebels, who, having trampled under foot, the Constitution of the
United States—the ark of our freedom and prosperity—are prepared to trample on the ashes of him to whom we are all mainly
indebted for those mighty blessings.

"Should the operations of war take the United States troops in
that direction, the General-in-chief does not doubt that each and
every man will approach with due reverence, and leave uninjured,
not only the tomb, but also the house, the groves and walks, which
were so loved by the best and greatest of men."

CHAPTER IX.

The following Song, written by a Dutch lady at the Hague, in 1779, for the sailors of five American vessels at Amsterdam, ought to be re-produced at this time, that it may never be forgotten by the American people as long as the days that tried men's souls are remembered—

God save the Thirteen States! long rule the United States!
    God save our States!
Make us victorious—happy and glorious,
No tyrant over us—God save our States.

Oft did America foresee with sad dismay,
    Her slavery near.
Oft did her grievance state, but Britain, falsely great,
Urging her desperate fate, turned a deaf ear.

Now the proud British foe, we've made, by victories, know,
    Our sacred right.
Witness at Bunker's Hill, where god-like Warren fell,
Happy his blood to spill, in gallant fight.

To our famed Washington—brave Starke at Bennington,
    Glory is due.
Peace to Montgomery's shade, who as he fought and bled,
Drew honors round his head, numerous and true.

View Saratoga's plain, our captures on the main,
    Moultrie's defence.
Our catalogue is long, of heroes yet unsung,
Who noble feats have done for Liberty.

The mother's melting moans, the aged father's groans,
    Have steeled our arms.
Ye British whigs beware ! your chains near formed are,
In spite of Richmond's care to sound alarms.

Come join your hands to ours ; no royal blocks, no towers,
    God save us all !
Thus in our country's cause, and to support our laws ;
Our swords shall never pause at Freedom's call.

We'll fear no tyrant's nod, no stern oppression's rod,
    Till time's no more.
Thus Liberty, when driven from Europe's states, is given
A safe retreat and haven, on our free shore.

O Lord, thy gifts in store, we pray on Congress pour,
    To guide our States.
May union bless our land, while we, with heart and hand,
Our mutual rights defend—God save our states !

God save the Thirteen States! long watch the prosperous fates,
    Over our States!
Make us victorious ! happy and glorious !
No tyrants over us ! God save our States !

The following songs, on account of their beautiful allusions to our
patriot fathers and to the flag, should be transmitted to posterity as
memorials of American patriotism still alive in the civil conflict of
1860.

OUR UNION.

The blood that flowed at Lexington, and crimsoned bright Champlain,
Streams still along the Southern Gulf, and by the Lakes of Maine ;
It flows in veins that swell above Pacific's golden sand,
And throbs in hearts that love and grieve by dark Atlantic's strand.

It binds in one vast brotherhood the trappers of the West
With men whose cities glass themselves in Erie's classic breast;
And those to whom September brings the fire-side's social hours
With those who see December's brow enwreathed with gorgeous
    flowers.

From where Columbia laughs to meet the smiling Western wave,
To where Potomac sighs beside the patriot hero's grave,
And from the streaming everglades to Huron's lordly flood,
The glory of a nation's past thrills through a kindred blood.

Wherever Arnold's tale is told, it dyes the cheek with shame
That glows with pride o'er Bunker's Hill or Moultrie's milder fame;
And wheresoe'er above the flag the stars of empire gleam,
Upon the deck, or o'er the dust, it pours a common stream.

It is a sacred legacy ye never can divide,
Nor take from village urchin, nor the son of city pride,
Nor the hunter's white-haired children, who find a fruitful home,
Where nameless lakes are sparkling, and where lonely rivers roam.

Greene drew his sword at Eutaw, and bleeding Southern feet
Ford the march across the Delaware, amid the snow and sleet;
And lo! upon the parchment where the natal record shines,
The burning page of Jefferson bears Franklin's calmer lines!

Can ye divide that record bright, and tear the names apart
That erst were written boldly there with plight of hand and heart?
Can ye erase a Hancock's name, e'en with the sabre's edge,
Or wash out with fraternal blood a Carroll's double pledge?

Say, can the South sell out her share in Bunker's hoary height?
Or can the North give up her boast of Yorktown's closing fight?
Can ye divide with equal hand a heritage of graves,
Or rend in twain the starry flag that o'er them proudly waves?

Can ye cast lots for Vernon's soil, or chaffer 'midst the gloom
That hangs its solemn folds around our common Father's tomb?
Or can ye meet around his grave as fratricidal foes,
Or make your burning curses o'er his pure and calm repose?

"Ye dare not !" is the Alleghanian thunder-toned decree,
'Tis echoed where Nevada guards the blue and tranquil sea,
Where tropic waves delighted clasp our flowery Southern shore,
And where through frowning mountain gates Nebraska's waters roar !

OUR COUNTRY'S FLAG.

BY A. W. BURKHART.

Come all ye sons of liberty, and join us in our song,
And to *Our Country* let us sing, "Our Country right or wrong."
When treason rears her hideous form, let patriots all unite
And battle for our country's flag, for liberty and right.
    Hurrah ! hurrah ! for liberty, hurrah !
    Hurrah for our country's flag, with *all* its stripes and stars.

The Union that *our father's* made in hallowed days of yore,
Foul treason strives to sever now, in falsehood, blood and war ;
Our patriot sires have gone to rest—a legacy they gave,
And let us now *united* be, the *sacred trust to save.*
    Hurrah ! hurrah ! for our father's flag, hurrah !
    Hurrah for the *red,* the *white,* the *blue,* with every radiant star.

Our country's flag, the patriot's pride—the symbol of the free ;
Oh, may it wave till time shall end, o'er every land and sea ;
May *tyrants* gaze upon its folds, with trembling fear dismayed,
'Till the oppressed of every clime are gathered 'neath its shade.
    Hurrah ! hurrah ! for liberty and right,
    Hurrah for freedom's glorious stripes and shining stars so bright.

'Twas borne aloft by Washington, in days of "seventy-six."
And Jackson brave, at New Orleans, new honors did affix ;
In Mexico, the gallant Scott fresh laurels did entwine—
The glorious flag of spangled stars, oh ! may they ever shine.
    Hurrah ! hurrah ! for the dear old flag, hurrah !
    'Twas fashioned by the *sainted dead, we'll not betray it now.*

'Twas consecrated by the blood of countless heroes slain—
Let us preserve its sacred folds free from dishonor's stain,

May curses seize the *traitor knave* who would its beauty mar,
Or strike from out its azure field a single precious star.
 Hurrah! hurrah! for the Union flag hurrah!
 Red, blue and white its stripes so bright, and its galaxy of stars.

Then may it wave o'er freedom's home its stripes of *red* and *white*
A thousand glorious years to come—posterity's delight,
Until, emblazoned on its blue, a hundred orbs shall shine,
And in one holy brotherhood, a hundred States combine.
 Hurrah! hurrah! for our country's flag hurrah!
 That banner bright, our heart's delight, begemmed with many
  a star.

"THREE HUNDRED THOUSAND MORE!"

BY W. C. BRYANT.

We are coming, "Father Abraham," three hundred thousand more,
From Mississippi's winding stream, and from New England's shore;
We leave our plows and workshops, our wives and children dear,
With hearts too full for utterance, but with a silent tear;
We dare not look behind us, but steadfastly before,
We are coming "Father Abraham," three hundred thousand more.

If you look across the hill-tops that meet the northern sky,
Long moving lines of rising dust your vision may descry,
And now the wind an instant tears that cloudy veil aside,
And floats aloft our spangled flag, in glory and in pride;
And bayonets in the sunlight gleam, and bands brave music pour,
We are coming "Father Abraham," three hundred thousand more.

If you look up all the valleys, where the growing harvests shine,
You may see our sturdy farmer boys fast forming into line;
And children from their mothers' knees are pulling at the weeds,
And learning how to reap and sow, against their country's needs;
And a farewell group stands weeping at every cottage door,
We are coming "Father Abraham," three hundred thousand more.

You have called us, and we're coming, by Richmond's bloody tide,
To lay us down for freedom's sake our brothers' bones beside,

Or from foul treason's treacherous hand to wrench the murderous
blade,
And in the face of foreign foes its fragments to parade;
Three hundred thousand loyal men, and true, have gone before,
We are coming "Father Abraham," three hundred thousand more.

We'll rally round our banner that waves and shines afar,
It is our patriot fathers' flag with every ancient star;
We'll all stand by the President until the victory's won,
Or fall beneath our flag to save the chair of Washington.
Six hundred thousand valiant men have volunteered before,
We are coming, "Father Abraham," three hundred thousand more.

www.ingramcontent.com/pod-product-compliance
Lightning Source LLC
Chambersburg PA
CBHW020755020726
47495CB00008B/2441